we loved its high-adrenaline action sequences and can't wait to see where this franchise goes next.

FILM INSIDER

A cursed jewel in the Dinoni crown

A crew member has confided to us that they are thinking of leaving the latest Rio Dinoni project, *The Forbidden Jewel*, due to safety concerns. Dramatic accidents seem to have plagued the production since the cast and crew arrived in Thailand last week. Luckily there have been no serious casualties on set so far, but it's been close. A spokesperson for Blake Saunders assured us that they are 'taking health and safety very seriously, and every guideline has been met'. If this is true, we can only assume that the production is experiencing a spell of rather bad luck. We're keeping our fingers crossed that this film makes it to cinemas in one piece.

Trailer Talk

To loving dads everywhere.

Especially to my wonderful dad, who always makes me feel like a superstar.

And to Graham, not only an amazing husband, but such a fun and adventurous dad.

OXFORD
UNIVERSITY PRESS

Great Clarendon Street, Oxford, OX2 6DP

Oxford University Press is a department of the University of Oxford.
It furthers the University's objective of excellence in research, scholarship,
and education by publishing worldwide. Oxford is a registered trade mark of
Oxford University Press in the UK and in certain other countries

Copyright © Tamsin Cooke 2018

The moral rights of the author have been asserted

Database right Oxford University Press (maker)

First published 2018

British Library Cataloguing in Publication Data
Data available

ISBN: 978-0-19-274984-0

1 3 5 7 9 10 8 6 4 2

Printed in Great Britain

Cover and inside illustration: lfH, Adehoidar/Shutterstock.com

STUNT DOUBLE

DOUBLE

JUNGLE CURSE

TAMSIN COOKE

OXFORD
UNIVERSITY PRESS

CHAPTER 1

I inhale sharply, sensing rather than seeing the fiery torch approach. I hear a *whoosh* and know I've been lit. The flames must be blazing down my back, over my legs. It's weird there's no heat. The fire builds, rumbling louder than a high-speed train. I'm supposed to do something, but what? My brain has frozen as if it can't quite believe I'm alight.

Then instinct kicks in.

I lurch towards fresh air, away from the smoke. Pumping my arms, I see they're covered in bright orange flames and I stumble faster as if I can outrun my limbs. Fire spreads to my stomach. I want to breathe, but I can't. It'll scorch my lungs. Suddenly I feel heat seep into the

1

back of my knee and remember my training. I belly-flop to the ground as if shot in the back. Fire extinguishers explode from all directions and a blanket's thrown over me. I lie still.

'You did it!' yells Seb, my instructor. 'You were a human torch.'

At last I dare to breathe.

'Tell me you got that on film,' I croak, clambering to my feet.

A cameraman grins from behind a tripod. 'Oh no. I forgot to press record.'

'Hah!'

'Are you all right or did you get burnt?' asks Seb.

'I dropped to the ground as soon as I felt some heat behind my knee.'

'Good, you did well.' He throws me a tube of cream. 'After your shower, rub that into the places that hurt. The awards ceremony is in about ninety minutes so you've got some time off. Right, Emma, you're up next,' he adds, turning to the next trainee.

I head for the washroom. It's a bit mad. Out of all the stunts I've done over the last two weeks, being set on fire was the easiest. I didn't really have to do anything. I just needed a team who made sure I was prepared and put the flames out afterwards. It's not like learning to fight with swords or rolling down spiral staircases. I yank off the gloves, my hood, and the many outer layers of clothes, then peel off the fire-retardant long underwear. I can't wait to get in the shower. My face and hair are covered in a special cooling gel and I bet I look like a blobfish.

*

Half an hour later, I return to the common room where most of my course mates are laughing and chatting. Grabbing a can of lemonade, I notice a newspaper lying open on a table. I stare at the headline and the temperature in the room seems to drop.

Is The Forbidden Jewel *heading for the cutting-room floor?*

I take the newspaper over to a corner where I can be alone and I read the article, my body growing colder and colder with each word.

Things are not looking good for the latest Rio Dinoni movie. Before filming's even begun, The Forbidden Jewel *is being plagued with strange incidents. Equipment's not working, crew members are failing to turn up, and, word has it, Vance Jackson—everyone's favourite villain—has been badly hurt and has had to pull out.*

Angus Strider, the director, is keen to say that everything's fine. They've had a few teething problems, but what movies haven't? And a spokesperson for teen Hollywood heart-throb Blake Saunders says, 'He's eager to start filming and take on the role of Dinoni again.'

But with rumours of disasters flying about, I'm wondering if this is another Ropen's Revenge, *the last*

3

Dinoni movie, which was shut down under suspicious circumstances. Action hero Rio might be able to save the world, but he can't seem to save his own films.

No, no, nooooo!

I stare at the article. I can't be in another failed film.

If this movie is cancelled, what was the point of me being set alight . . . or even being here? And this film looks like it's going to be even better than the last one. Rio's on a mission to stop an ancient sect of Thai warriors from stealing the Queen's Sapphire. I might get to use swords and do ninja-style fighting.

'You all right, Finn? You look shocked.'

I tear my eyes away from the paper to find Calum Somwan standing in front of me. Unlike the rest of my course mates who are at least four years older, he's only eighteen and for some reason thinks he's God's gift to the planet.

'Is it because you finally passed a stunt?' he asks with a sneer.

'What are you talking about? I passed them all.'

'Really? What about the horse stunt?'

My stomach squirms. I've been trying to forget that one. 'All right, you got me. I'm not good with horses, but I've only ever ridden once before. Some of us haven't had riding lessons all our lives.'

Calum smirks. 'I don't think I'll ever forget your face when that horse started trotting.'

'It didn't trot, it galloped. Anyway, I don't have to be good on horses. I chose bikes and cars.'

'Some of us are good at all the stunts.' He tilts his head. 'Some of us don't just scrape by.'

'I didn't just scrape by,' I say. *Why do I let him get to me?* He raises his eyebrow, and I grab my can, snapping back the tab. 'But tell me, Calum, exactly how many stunts have you performed in a film? And not just during this course so you can get a tick in the box. I mean on actual movie sets?'

'Like you have?' he says.

Argh! How I'd love to see his face if he knew I was the stunt double for Blake Saunders; that I was in *The Ropen's Revenge*; and that I'm about to be in *The Forbidden Jewel*. I hate secrecy contracts, but the world must think Blake does his own stunts.

Calum shakes his head. 'I don't know why you're even here.'

'I could say the same about you,' I lie.

'Loser,' he mutters before turning away, joining the rest of our course.

I sip my lemonade, hardly tasting it. Have I really been that bad? Because I have to pass this course or Strider won't let me be in the film. Surely if I've failed, someone would have told me by now. They wouldn't be waiting to announce it at the awards ceremony in front of an audience.

Would they?

5

CHAPTER 2

Half an hour later, we're sitting in one of the larger rooms for the awards ceremony. I'm in the second row, surrounded by course mates and as far away from Calum as possible. Friends and family members seep into the room, but there's no sign of Mum. I just hope she managed to get some time off work. Soon the chairs behind us fill up and I keep looking out for her platinum curls, but Mum's still not here when Seb heads to the front.

'I can't believe you motley crew passed,' he says with a wink. Then he looks at each of us in turn. 'Actually, you all deserve it.'

We all *deserve it . . . which means I passed. Yesssss!*

'You've worked incredibly hard,' says Seb. 'You learnt to fight, fall, roll, play dead. You've driven bikes and cars, swum in tanks, and been set on fire. So it is with great pleasure that I introduce you to our patron, who will be handing out the certificates today.'

The door opens and Mum rushes inside, carrying a massive bag. She stops, her eyes widening as she sees the audience.

'Not quite who I was expecting,' says Seb, and everyone laughs.

I lift my hand into the air, and give her a half-hearted wave.

She clasps a hand to her chest sheepishly. 'Sorry I'm late.'

'We're just glad you made it,' says Seb. 'You should be very proud of your son.'

'I always am,' says Mum, finding a seat at the back.

Seb smiles. 'So now, let me introduce you to our patron.'

A side door opens and it's as if the air is sucked right out of the room. Marcus Saunders strides inside. *He* is the patron? How did I not know this? People shift in their seats, some scrabbling for mobiles to take pictures or videos. Marcus Saunders is Blake's movie-star dad, he's won a ton of awards in the industry, and is fancied by every woman on the planet, including my mum. I used to see him when I was younger, but now not so much. It's weird seeing him in the flesh again, when I'm used to seeing him on the big screen. It's like I forgot he was real.

Marcus smiles his trademark grin and I think I actually hear swooning. Glancing back at mum, her cheeks are bright pink.

'I see you *may* have noticed who our patron is,' says Seb with a chuckle. 'We're very lucky to have Marcus with us today. If it were next week, he'd be in Thailand filming the next Rio Dinoni film.'

I join in the clapping, but my mind is buzzing. *He's in The Forbidden Jewel too?*

'Thank you for the warm welcome,' says Marcus, his rich voice filling the room. 'It is such an honour to be here. Stunt performers are the unsung heroes— doing the stunts we actors are too afraid to try. You have amazing coordination and bravery. And Seb is right— I will be in Thailand. I wasn't supposed to be, but Vance Jackson who was playing the villain has broken his leg.'

So . . . some of the rumours are true then!

'A huge congratulations to all of you,' adds Marcus. 'I know this course is tough.'

We applaud him again and Seb steps forward. 'OK, everyone. I'm going to announce the top trainee of the course. This is the person who has the right attitude, tried the hardest, and achieved the impossible. The rest of you will be called out afterwards but please be aware you are in no order of ranking.'

8

He clears his throat and I grip the edge of my seat. I've tried really hard. But if it's not me, whatever happens, don't let it be—

'Calum Somwan, could you please come to the front?' says Seb.

Of all the people!

We clap. Well, I pretend to, my palms not quite making contact. Calum swaggers to the front, like he's some sort of 'heavy' from a gangster film.

'I guess I'm made of stronger stuff,' he says, pumping his arms, and I half expect him to kiss his biceps.

People laugh. I want to be sick. Marcus shakes his hand and then leans in, whispering something. The smug smile on Calum's face grows even bigger. He throws his fist into the air before returning to his seat. Then Seb runs through the rest of the names and one by one my course mates get their certificates.

'And last, but by no means least, we have Finn Gibson, who in spite of his age has managed to keep up with everyone.'

Hear that Calum?

Working my way along the row, I avoid my course mates' feet, but as I pass Calum sitting on the end, I trip over his foot. He grins, whipping his leg back in. *That little—*

'What were you saying about coordination?' says Calum loudly, and a few people snicker.

Scrambling to my feet, my face burns. Calum's eyes

glint with menace and I know he's taunting me, wanting me to blame him so I sound like a child. I'm not giving him that satisfaction.

I hold out my arms. 'And that, ladies and gentlemen, is called a stunt stumble,' I say, taking a bow, and people laugh again, but this time with me rather than at me.

I reach the front and Marcus beams, shaking my hand. 'It is with great pleasure I pass on this certificate to Finn. I have known him for years. He is good friends with my son. They went to drama club together.'

My course mates look at me in surprise, apart from Calum. He looks like he's plotting all the different ways to kill me. I try to find Mum when I notice Blake grinning at the back of the room. Whoa! What's he doing here?

'Considering his age, I think you'll all agree, Finn's done incredibly well,' continues Marcus. 'I don't know of any other fourteen-year-old who could do half of this.'

For a split second, Blake's grin drops. Then it's back in full force. 'Maybe the rest of us fourteen-year-olds are too smart,' says Blake. 'Finn *chose* to be set on fire.'

Everyone laughs and turns. Then their mouths drop open and their phones are out again, although this time pointing at Blake. My shoulders slump; like always, the spotlight swings to him.

'Blake wanted to be here to support you,' whispers Marcus. Then he grabs hold of my hand, lifts it into the air, and says, 'Finn.'

Suddenly Mum leaps to her feet, clapping and cheering wildly. You'd have thought I'd won an Oscar. *Why mum? WHY???* I step away, dying to disappear.

'No, wait,' she cries, rummaging through her bag. 'I haven't got a good picture yet.'

I stand at the front, my cheeks burning as if I am on fire again.

'You've got to love mums,' whispers Marcus.

'Even when they do this?'

'Especially when they do this,' he says with a chuckle.

While mum snaps away, I desperately want Blake to be the centre of attention again.

CHAPTER

3

As soon as the ceremony's finished, I head over to Blake.

'I would not have missed that for the world. I could have fried eggs on your face,' he says.

I wince. 'What are you doing here, anyway?'

'I have to make sure my stunt double is worthy of me,' he whispers with a grin. Then says louder, 'Actually, after this, we're going for dinner to celebrate Dad getting the part of the villain. We're meeting Mum at The Hilton.'

'Caviar and champagne, then?'

'Well, of course,' he says snootily. 'To be honest, I'd much rather have pizza.'

I feel a hand on my shoulder and turn to find Calum. For some strange reason he's smiling at me.

'Well done, mate, you were amazing on this course,' he says.

Wait? What?

'Didn't you come top of the group?' Blake asks him.

Calum's hand drops from my shoulder and he shrugs bashfully. 'I think it was just luck.'

Who is this person? Has he had a brain transplant somewhere between now and five minutes ago?

'Blake, I just wanted to say,' continues Calum, 'I saw that footage of you jumping off Tower Bridge for *The Ropen's Revenge.* You were really good.'

Blake glances at me, his lips twitching. 'It was nothing. Quite easy, really.'

Seriously? That was me! I jumped off Tower Bridge and it was not nothing. It was scary and freezing and I didn't have any safety equipment. But of course I can't say anything.

Calum tilts his head. 'I don't suppose you'd sign an autograph for my little sister?'

'Why lie, Calum? We know you're an only child,' I snap, before leaving them to it.

I find Mum, who's looking rather awkward. 'I'm really sorry, love, but I've got to leave,' she says. 'I only got a few hours off work and it's late closing tonight.'

'I'll come with you.'

'No, you stay and celebrate.'

'I'd much rather come with you.'

She beams and together we walk out of the academy, passing the Saunder's limo parked on the side of the road. We take the Tube across London and then I walk her to the hair salon.

'So I thought we could get a take-out pizza tonight to celebrate,' she says. I open my mouth. 'And before you ask—yes, we can afford it.'

I smile. 'That would be great, Mum. Thanks.'

Then she looks over my shoulder and scowls. 'Your friend is here.'

I turn to see Sam walking towards me.

'Just promise me one thing,' whispers Mum. 'Don't get into trouble. You're flying out tomorrow and I don't want you to do anything to jeopardize that. And don't be late home. I need to dye your hair again. Turn you back into Blake.'

I pull a face. 'Don't remind me.'

'Be good,' warns Mum, before walking into the salon.

'I don't think she likes me,' says Sam.

'She does. She just thinks you're a bad influence.'

'Me? You're the one always getting us into trouble.'

I shrug. 'What are you doing here, anyway?'

'I'm on my way to the park. Mel and Carla are there,' he says, his face breaking into a grin. 'You coming?'

'You know you don't have a chance with them.'

'You say that, but—'

For the entire journey, Sam tells me exactly how one

of them will fall madly in love with him. He doesn't care which one.

'Oh, you're kidding,' I groan.

For Mel and Carla aren't alone. They're sitting on the swings while Sam's older brother Ollie and another boy I don't recognize lean against the posts.

'Should we go?' I say, but I'm too late. They've spotted us.

'Hey, if it isn't my little brother and his ballet-dancing pal.'

'I don't ballet dance,' I say.

'No? Then where've you been for the last two weeks?' says Ollie.

'At drama school,' I say, glancing at Sam for back-up. I've been telling that story to my best friend for the past few months. If he knew I was really a stunt double, the whole world would know in less than three minutes. And it wouldn't take long for people to work out that I'm doubling Blake—the all-action superstar. But Sam isn't even listening. He's looking at the girls, swaggering towards them like some sort of gorilla on steroids.

'That's not what our mum says. She says you've been doing ballet and that's why you're so secretive,' says Ollie.

Mel and Carla giggle.

'I'm not a ballet dancer!'

The other boy pushes himself off the post. 'Aren't you Finn Gibson?'

I nod warily.

15

'You're the one who won that motorbike race?' he says.

'Which one?'

'You ride motorbikes?' says Carla, looking at me with new interest.

I have for years. One of Mum's boyfriends taught me.

Sam's eyes dart between her and me. 'He's the best,' he says quickly. 'Could beat anyone.'

'Then race me now,' says the boy.

'I don't have a bike.'

'You can borrow mine.' Ollie points to a motorbike in the car park—small, blue and covered in scratches. I recognize it straight away.

'Does your uncle know you've got it?' I ask.

Ollie smirks. 'Not exactly.'

'So what do you say? Do you want a race?' asks the boy.

'He wouldn't dare, Tyler. He wants to go home and find his tutu,' says Ollie, and the girls giggle again.

'All right. I'm in.'

CHAPTER 4

Clutching the keys in my hand, I swing my leg over the bike. 'Where are we racing?'

'To Dave's fish and chip shop.' Tyler climbs onto the bigger bike next to mine, while Sam hands me a helmet.

'And back?' I say.

'No. Just one way. Then we'll do it again.'

Mel pulls off her jacket, her eyes sparkling. 'I'll start the race. I don't have a scarf, but I'll use this.'

She stands to the side of us, waving her jacket high in the air. I turn the key in the ignition, press the power button, and twist the throttle. The engine roars to life, vibrating beneath me. Tyler revs his bike even louder.

Mel brings down her arm and I release the clutch, shooting out of the car park. I hurtle down the road, the engine roaring in my ears, the wind tearing through my T-shirt. I'm not wearing a jacket. If I fall off, it's going to hurt even more than normal. Leaning into the bend, my back wheel drifts around the corner when Tyler cuts me off. I squeeze the brakes and my motorbike skids beneath me. Slamming my foot down, at least I'm upright, but now Tyler's out of sight. Twisting the throttle again, I race down the street and take the next left. To my relief, the traffic lights up ahead are red and Tyler's at the front. Weaving in and out of the queuing cars, I crank up the speed and burst through the junction just as the lights turn green. We're neck and neck. I lean forward and bend sharply. I spot the chippie. I overtake a lorry and a horn blares. But I don't care. I skid to a stop, seconds before Tyler.

Pulling off my helmet, I say, 'I guess I won.'

'Only cos of the traffic lights,' he says, whipping off his helmet as well.

'It doesn't matter. I still—'

'Finlay Gibson, what are you doing on that bike?'

My stomach drops as I turn my head.

'Mum,' I yelp.

Tyler sniggers beside me but in the next second, his engine rips through the air. While Mum storms towards me, I watch Tyler and his bike disappear. If only I could do the same.

'I thought you were at work,' I say.

'I bet you did. But they let me off early so I could celebrate with you.'

By the look on her face, I think we're no longer celebrating.

'That was nice of them,' I say.

Her eyes narrow to flints.

'Whose bike is that?' she demands.

'Sam's uncle's.'

'Does he know you have it?'

I shake my head.

'So you stole a motorbike and went for a ride?'

'I didn't steal it. Ollie—I mean, I—borrowed it.'

'And you went racing? You were the two fools I saw at the traffic lights.' She shakes her head. 'What were you thinking? What if the police had caught you? You'd be off the film. What if you hurt someone? What if you hurt yourself? In fact, were you even thinking at all?'

I look at the ground.

'Did I or did I not tell you to keep out of trouble?'

'You did,' I mumble.

'I'm sorry, I can't quite hear you,' she says, spit flying from her lips.

'You did,' I say louder.

'Right.' She crosses her arms. 'You need to get that bike back to Sam's uncle and then you and I will continue this conversation back at home.'

I nod and turn on the ignition.

'Oh no! You're not riding it. That's illegal. You're pushing it.'

'But he lives miles away.'

'Not my problem,' says Mum.

'What happens if the police see me pushing it? They'll ask questions.'

'Then you can tell them that you are pushing it because you know you are too young to ride it.' She looks at me with such venom there's no point in arguing. 'You will walk it all the way and apologize to his uncle.'

'I can't do that,' I yelp. 'That'll land Ollie and Sam in it. Their uncle will go mad and he's not there, anyway.' At least I don't think he is, otherwise they wouldn't have *borrowed* his bike.

Mum's lips smack together. 'All right, you don't have to apologize. But you do have to walk the bike. Don't you dare get on it. I will see you when you get home.'

With a sigh, I traipse though the streets, pushing the bike as if I was taking a dog for a walk—a heavy reluctant dog that doesn't want to move. I think about getting on the bike, but if she found out, I would be deader than a ghost.

By the time I get home, I'm hot, sweaty, aching, and starving. I bet Mum's changed her mind about pizza. We're probably having baked potato and beans. But as I push open the door, the delicious smells of pepperoni, melting cheese, and crisp baked bread rush towards me. *Thank you, Mum.*

I hear her say goodbye to someone. Walking into the kitchen, Mum's leaning against the counter, the phone in her hands and a very strange expression on her face. The pizza boxes haven't been opened. Oh God—was that the police?

'Strider was on the phone,' she says, as if in a trance.

'Strider? The director?'

She nods and my heart starts pounding.

'You're not flying out tomorrow.'

It's like the world is crumbling. 'They don't want me?' I whisper.

Her face breaks into a giant grin. 'Oh no, they want you all right. But you're flying out the day after with Marcus, Natasha, and Blake on their private jet.'

'Are you serious?'

She nods.

'I am going on a private jet?' *Me? Finn Gibson, who's only ever been abroad once before and that was for another film.* I punch the air with my fists. Then my arms drop to my sides. 'Did you say Natasha's going?'

The smile on Mum's face thins. 'She's got some time off work and wants it to be a family affair.' Natasha is an actor too and has won possibly even more awards than Marcus. She thinks I'm far too poor and common to be friends with her precious son.

'She hates me,' I say.

'Well, obviously not, otherwise you wouldn't be going with them.'

'Why am I going with them?' I ask suddenly. 'I thought I was supposed to be going with my stunt team.'

'Plans change,' says Mum, shrugging.

And I beam again. Who cares why? I am going on a private jet. I'll be extra polite to Natasha. Who knows? She might even grow to like me. I squeeze past our table to get two plates out of the cupboard. 'You know what, Mum? I'm going to work really hard, so one day I'll be taking you on a private jet.'

'I look forward to it.' she says with a warm smile. Then it disappears. 'But don't think for one minute I haven't forgotten about your motorbike ride.'

'At least I didn't get back on the bike. I pushed it all the way.'

'I should hope so!' she says. 'And as you're not flying out tomorrow, you can spend the day helping me clean the house.'

'What?'

'Think of it as your punishment.'

I kind of wish I was going with the stunt team now, but I nod meekly, dropping into my chair. There's no point trying to get out of this one. She opens the boxes to reveal one pepperoni and one ham and pineapple—our favourites.

'Sam's mum came into the salon yesterday,' she says, popping some pineapple into her mouth. 'She asked why she hasn't seen you around for the last two weeks, so I told her you've been busy.'

'Doing what?'

'Going to ballet school.'

I stare at Mum without blinking. 'Tell me you're joking.'

'No. What's wrong with ballet? I knew a lot of male ballet dancers when I was younger and they were so strong and fit, just like you.'

I grab a piece of pizza but suddenly it doesn't look quite as appetising. Then my phone pings with a one-word message from Sam.

Loser!

I quickly type back: *Hey—I won the race.*

Tyler said he did.

Tyler's a liar.

Is your mum mad at you?

I have to clean the house tomorrow.

She hasn't told my mum, has she?

Don't think so.

I'll see you Monday then.

Actually, I'm being sent out of the country. Mum thinks you're a really bad influence so she's sending me to military school.

Military school—yeah, right! We all know you're going to ballet camp . . .

'Finn, no phones allowed at the table!' snaps Mum.

CHAPTER 5

Less than forty-eight hours later, I'm on the Saunders' private jet. It's almost as big as a commercial airliner and can fly all the way to Thailand without refuelling. Instead of being crammed with people, it has four passengers and about five times as many aircrew. I can't quite believe I'm here. I feel like I'm in a James Bond movie rather than in real life. There are actual bedrooms, at least three times the size of mine back home, with hotel-style double beds covered in faux-fur cushions and satin sheets. There's a lounge with corner sofas, armchairs, a mini-bar, and a dining area. Enormous flat-screen TVs line partition walls and have PlayStations attached.

We've already been flying for nine hours and I've hardly seen Marcus and Natasha: only when we first arrived and met on the plane. While the press followed Blake and his parents through the airport, I snuck on board with the aircrew, huddled in between them so no one could catch a glimpse of me. Not that the press would pay any attention to me anyway.

Blake puts down his PlayStation controller. 'I hope this film is going to be a little less exciting than last time.'

'What? You're hoping that Strider doesn't turn out to be a maniac director who will kill anyone who gets in the way of his precious film?'

Blake laughs. 'And I'm really hoping he doesn't dump us in the middle of a jungle so you can capture a mythological creature.'

'That isn't that mythological.'

'How's your back?'

'It's fine. There are still some scars but they don't hurt.'

When I freed the Ropen—a pterodactyl-type creature—its claws scraped through me and neon blue gunk from its underbelly seeped into my wounds. I've never felt pain like it and afterwards I kept hallucinating, seeing random creatures like dragons and fire squirrels.

'Have you heard from Mawi at all?' asks Blake. She's the girl from Papua New Guinea who was dumped in the jungle with us.

'We messaged a couple of times, but we've kind of drifted apart.'

'Kind of? You live on opposite ends of the world. I don't think you could be any more apart.'

'Thanks!'

'What are friends for?' he says lifting up his remote, about to start again.

I bite my lip. 'Blake, why am I here with you instead of my stunt team? I thought I was flying out with them.'

'I don't think they wanted you,' he says with a grin. 'In all honesty, Dad wanted me entertained. He thought if I had you with me, he wouldn't have to play computer games all the way and he could stay in his suite with Mum.'

'So . . . I'm basically your toy?'

'I'd go with android. Now why don't you pick up your remote control like a good little robot and let me beat you for the hundredth time?'

'You couldn't beat me if I was blindfolded,' I say, choosing my new character in the game. 'And just so you know, I'm playing because I want to. Not because I'm your toy.'

'I could give you a name—Blake's Entertainment Android.'

'And I could give you a black eye,' I say.

✻

By the time the plane arrives at the airport, I'm exhausted. Perhaps I should have tried to get some sleep rather than play for twelve solid hours. Blake disappears off to his

26

room for a few minutes and comes back wearing fresh clothes and hair gel. Even though we're pretty much the same height and build and now have the same hair colour, he looks like a Hollywood heart-throb and I look like a scarecrow.

'My fans might be out there,' he explains with a shrug. 'I can't let them down.'

'You are so vain.' Then I spot a flight attendant grab my bag. 'Do I need to get off with the aircrew?'

But this time I'm escorted off with Blake, Marcus, and Natasha. Large men in black suits fetch us from the aircraft and walk us through security. All I want to do is get to my bed but travellers stop what they're doing and pull out their phones. Some ask for selfies, while others thrust paper and pen into the Saunders' hands. I'm barged aside again and again, as Blake and his family show endless patience for their fans. Part of me feels irritated. The other part—a secret part—wishes just one person would ask me for my autograph.

'We need to get a move on,' says one of the security guards at last. 'Someone will have tipped off the paparazzi by now.'

Those are the magic words.

Natasha nods and suddenly we're surrounded by guards, as they bustle us through the arrivals lounge. The automatic doors open and, even though it's about nine o'clock at night, the heat of Thailand hits me straight away. We're led over to a gleaming black limousine and, as I climb inside, I relish the air conditioning. The limo rolls out of the airport, but as it's dark outside, I hardly see a thing. Marcus switches on a light in the cabin and Natasha helps herself to a glass of champagne.

'Would you boys like a drink?' she asks.

We nod. She passes us a Coke each, beaming at Blake, her smile tightening a little when she looks at me.

'Thank you ever so much,' I say, remembering to be polite.

'So, Finn, I've been watching your stunts from *The Ropen's Revenge*, and I have to say I'm very impressed,' says Marcus. 'You were incredibly brave.'

Beside me, Blake stiffens.

'Some would say I was stupid.'

I'm sure Natasha nods, as she looks out of the window.

'Dad,' says Blake, rubbing the back of his neck. 'I was wondering, now that you're working on this film, do you think Strider would let me do a few more of my own stunts?'

Marcus's face lights up. 'I can ask him. That's a great idea.'

Natasha's head whips back around. 'I'm not sure Strider will agree. What if something happens to him?'

'Strider will be fine. Why don't you admit it? You don't want anything to happen to him.'

'Is it such a bad thing that I want to keep our son safe?'

Suddenly I think of Mum. Is she even worried about me?

'Strider wouldn't allow either boy to hurt themselves,' says Marcus. 'Everything will be properly set up with safety precautions and the right equipment.'

'But Finn is properly trained. He's been on a stunt course,' says Natasha.

Thankfully the conversation fades and I look out of the window. I can't see anything apart from a few lights scattered amongst the blackness. But as we near the town, shops, houses, and beautiful golden temples are lit up. We hit traffic and this gives me a better chance to glimpse the side streets. They're filled with market stalls. Smoke rises from grills and I can see railings of clothes, paintings, and masks. The place is teeming with people, on foot or hanging off mopeds. Families of four squeeze onto one bike, buzzing in between stalls and cars, narrowly missing each other.

'Welcome to Hiva Hin,' says Marcus.

Blake pulls a face. 'Tell me we're not staying here.'

'Why not? It's fabulous,' I say.

'No, five-star accommodation is fabulous.' Blake winks as if he's joking but I'm not sure he is.

Twisting and turning through the town, we leave the markets and shopping centres far behind. We reach an area full of houses, with a few restaurants and street vendors scattered about. We stop at the end of a long road, where a gate and a security cabin block our way. A security guard jumps out and our limo driver opens his window. The blast of hot air rushes into the back.

Natasha tuts. 'He could at least have closed our compartment first.'

But I'm glad it's open. I listen to them talk in what I assume is Thai, and soon we're ushered through. Bungalows line the side streets and the main road, and dogs seem to be everywhere. I think they must be strays.

'The producers have booked all these houses. The camera crew are in that one,' says Marcus, pointing to the nearest bungalow, 'and you and your stunt team are a few streets down.'

'Where are you staying?' I ask.

'A little further on,' says Marcus.

We pull up beside a bungalow identical to the others. The lights shine through the blinds, so I know people are in. I climb out and the chauffeur grabs my suitcase from the boot and drops it to the ground with a thud. Bet he wouldn't do that to the Saunders' luggage! Luckily I have nothing valuable inside.

I watch the black car slip away before walking up the driveway, dragging my bag behind. So this is it. The moment I meet my stunt team. I take a deep breath and knock on the door. A few seconds later, I hear footsteps and the door opens. My heart drops faster than my suitcase.

What the hell is *he* doing here?

CHAPTER

6

Calum stands in the doorway. 'Surprised to see me?'

'What are you doing here?'

He smirks. 'When Marcus Saunders found out how good I was at the academy, he had to have me.'

'They happened to need someone with your looks and height. You got lucky,' says a short stocky man with a broad Scottish accent and a mop of greying hair. He pushes Calum to one side and grabs my suitcase. 'I'm Jenks. You must be Finn Gibson. Come in, but take your shoes off first.'

I kick off my battered trainers and follow him into a large open-plan room. Paintings of Thailand cover the walls and there are different-sized sculptures of Buddha on bookshelves. The whir of air conditioning fills the room and playing cards cover the breakfast counter. Two men and a woman lie sprawled across the sofas, watching TV. They must be at least twenty-five.

'Everyone, our last member has arrived,' says Jenks. 'This is Finn.'

They turn their heads and instantly get to their feet.

'Welcome to Thailand, Finn,' says an American shaven-headed man with a goatee beard. He looks like he should be on a Harley Davidson driving through the desert.

The woman smiles warmly. 'So you're the fourteen-year-old everyone's talking about. I'm Lucy.'

'And I'm Tom,' says another man. 'I'm so impressed you passed that course.'

Calum snorts but I choose to ignore him.

'Our team is complete,' says Jenks, clasping my shoulder. 'Just so you know, I am your stunt coordinator. Think of me as your friend and boss, though not necessarily in that order. As you're underage, you need a guardian. Richie will be with you at all times. He's being doing stunts for years.'

'And I am more than happy to help,' says the shaven-headed man.

'Now I imagine you want to go to bed after that flight unless you want something to eat,' says Jenks.

'Bed sounds good.'

He smiles kindly. 'You've got tomorrow to get acclimatized as well; you don't start filming until the day after. But as we're all involved in the scenes, I think you're spending the day with Marcus and Blake. We can't leave you alone.'

'Aw, he needs a babysitter,' says Calum so quietly that only I can hear.

Jenks suddenly looks a little sheepish. 'Now, I am afraid to say, as you were the last one here, you get the last choice of the room. And when I say last choice, I mean no choice.'

'That's all right,' I say. I mean ... how bad can it be?

'Calum will show you where everything is.'

I follow Calum into a hallway and he opens a door halfway down. The room's much larger than mine back at home and has a double bed, sofa, desk, and TV. It looks brilliant. I step inside when Calum tugs me back.

'This is mine,' he says with a glint in his eyes. 'You're at the end of the corridor.'

With a growing sense of unease, I follow him again. He opens another door and I step inside. He couldn't join me even if he wanted to. There's a single bed—if you can call it that—which looks like it was made for a five-year-old. Plus a wardrobe. That's it. No chair, desk or TV. At the back of the room is an air-conditioning unit with a fork sticking out of it.

'Don't touch the fork or the air conditioning will stop. And the bathroom's next door. Some of the bedrooms have en suites, but where would yours go?'

I close the door, but can still hear Calum sniggering. The room seems to shrink even more. I flop onto the bed, but to fit on I have to bend my legs. I can't even dangle my feet over the edge because a wall is there. This seems really unfair. I am Rio's stunt double. Surely I should have a bigger room. *Oh no!* I force myself to stop. I'm obviously spending far too much time with Blake. I'm turning into him.

✳

I wake up to noises outside my room and imagine everyone's getting ready to go. Thank God I don't have to get up. I turn over in bed when there's a knock on my door.

'Sorry, dude, I've got to take you to the Thai Orchid.'

'The Thai what?' I ask blearily, opening the door.

'The Thai Orchid,' says Richie. 'It's a restaurant the producers have hired to feed the film crew. Marcus should be there waiting for you.'

'What time is it?'

'Seven. So not early. Although you're probably in a mixed-up time zone right now.'

'Do I have time for a shower?'

'You have ten minutes.'

I'm ready in six. It's only a three-minute walk to the restaurant, but I shouldn't have bothered with a shower.

My back's dripping by the time we arrive. I follow Richie inside, savouring the air conditioning. Spices fly up my nose and I stare at the buffet counters filled with meats, soups, and rice. Strange choices for breakfast but they smell delicious and my stomach rumbles. There are lots of square wooden tables in the middle and I spot Blake and Marcus straight away. It's not hard. The rest of the film crew are trying not to look at them. Richie leaves as Marcus waves me over.

'Good morning, Finn,' he says, as if he hasn't spent half the night flying.

Blake looks a little more how I feel: bags under his eyes and his hair flatter than usual.

'Why don't you get some food and then we can head to the studios? I thought we could take a look around,' says Marcus.

I join the short queue at the nearest counter, when a woman in front of me says, 'You're joking, right? Someone *actually* stole the scaffolding? How do you steal scaffolding?'

'I don't know,' says a man. 'But it was there last night, and then, this morning all of it's gone. Strider's furious. He thinks someone should have seen something, but if they have, they're not saying.'

Aware I'm staring, I quickly look past them, pretending to concentrate on a painting of a lion with flamed hooves and a monkey with glowing eyes.

The woman shakes her head. 'How many more

things can go wrong with this film before they decide to shut it down?'

'Don't say that, I need this job,' says the man.

No, don't say that!

I help myself to a bowl of chicken and rice, while their words go round and around my brain. Falling into the seat next to Blake, I say, 'There's no way Strider will stop this film is there?'

Marcus chuckles. 'Don't listen to rumours. This film is fine.'

'This film is just perfect,' snaps Blake.

I turn to him in surprise. 'What's up?' I whisper out of the corner of my mouth.

'Families,' he mutters, glaring at his dad.

But Marcus doesn't seem to notice. He talks cheerfully throughout breakfast and in the limo to the studios. I thought we'd be leaving the secure complex but it turns out the producers have hired some warehouses further down from the bungalows. Climbing out, we walk past a bunch of movie trailers and head for the nearest warehouse.

'They've all been soundproofed,' says Marcus, pulling out a set of keys. His eyes gleam. 'And I have keys to everything.'

He opens the door and the roar of motorbikes hits me. I forget about the rumours of the film and about Blake being quiet. Staring at the film set, my heart starts pounding.

'Please tell me Rio gets to use this,' I say.

Marcus shakes his head. 'Sadly not. This is for the villains only.'

What???

'I don't want to play Rio anymore. Can I be a bad guy?' I ask.

CHAPTER 7

I gaze at the building. An outdoor staircase runs up the side and a sign saying *Wall of Death* dangles off the front. I've seen these on TV but never in real life before.

'Are they filming inside?'

'I wouldn't have brought you here if they were,' says Marcus. 'The riders are practising.'

I glance at Blake. He's not sulking any more. In fact he looks like how I feel.

'Can we watch?' I ask and Marcus nods.

Blake and I sprint up the stairs, open a door, and end up on a viewing platform that runs around the perimeter of the room. We peer over. The room below is like a barrel: a vertical wooden wall leading to a flat floor slightly ramped around the ring at the bottom. A man and woman ride on motorbikes horizontally halfway up the wall without helmets or holding the handlebars. They whisk around and around. It doesn't look possible. Marcus joins us and together we watch them circle the inside of the cylinder.

'How do they do that?' I whisper.

'I think they have to be a certain speed and then gravity keeps them in place,' says Marcus.

The riders go higher and higher as if they're on an invisible helter-skelter until one of them is only about two foot below us. Each time she passes, I feel a whoosh of air. Then they descend again, spiralling down, driving over the ramp until they're on the flat floor. They cut their engines, and Blake and I burst into applause. Looking up, they grin and bow their heads. Then they climb off their motorbikes and disappear through a door hidden in the wall.

'I need to talk to them about a scene. I'll be back in about fifteen minutes,' says Marcus. 'You can go into the actual room if you like.'

We leave the balcony and climb down the external staircase. While Marcus goes to find the riders outside, Blake and I locate the other door and soon we're standing in the centre of the barrel. The vertical wall seems even steeper from the inside.

'I think we should write in a scene where Rio has to ride in here,' I say.

'You know you couldn't do it. They've probably had years of training.' Then Blake looks at me sharply. 'Don't take that as a dare.'

'I won't,' I say . . .

Except I can't stand people saying that I can't do things. Plus the keys are in the ignition—it's as if they're inviting me to have a go—and when am I ever going to get another chance to do this? Marcus said they'll be about a quarter of an hour. Before I know it, I'm swinging my leg over a bike.

'Finn!' shouts Blake in horror.

'Stand in the middle, out of the way,' I say, turning on the engine, pressing the power button.

I twist the throttle and sweep around the base of the room, then edge my way onto the ramp. The ramp isn't steep, but the wall . . . *Come on, Finn, you've got this!* Blake waves his arms madly, wanting me to stop, but time is running out. Adrenalin screams through my veins as I touch the vertical wall. But my tyre slips and I crash down to the ground. I leap out of the way, sliding across the floor, before the bike can crush me.

'Finn!'

That's not Blake.

I look up to find Marcus leaning over the balcony and even from up here I see the fury in his eyes. Blake hurries over, picking up the bike.

'It's not broken,' he says, giving it a once over.

'Neither am I. Just in case you're concerned,' I say, standing up.

Glancing back at the balcony Marcus has disappeared. Then he bursts through the side door. 'Tell me you're OK.'

'I'm fine,' I say.

He looks at me and swallows. I think he's trying to get his breathing under control. 'Do you realize how seriously you could have been hurt?'

'I just . . . I wanted a go.'

'I thought I could trust you. I thought I could leave you alone. Do I have to hold your hand to make sure you behave?'

I lower my head.

'What if you'd wrecked the bike or the set in some way?'

'I don't think I have.' I look at Blake. 'The bike is all right, isn't it?'

'It's fine,' he says.

Marcus runs his hands through his hair, his eyes darting to the ceiling. 'When I heard that bike engine, I thought, *Finn's gone and*—' He shakes his head.

'I'm sorry,' I say.

He exhales loudly and suddenly his lips twitch. 'What was it like?'

'It was great, although I couldn't do it.'

He turns to his son. 'Did you have a go?'

'No.'

'Of course you didn't,' says Marcus, and if I'm not mistaken, disappointment edges into his voice.

Blake winces. 'Some of us know how to behave professionally.'

'Yep, you are always very sensible and trustworthy.'
Marcus swings his arm around his son. 'Right, we should
get out of here.'

I follow the pair out through the side door, when I
hear a bang. Darting back into the ring, I look up at the
balcony and spot a shadow move. Oh no! Did someone
else see me ride that bike? Am I going to get into trouble?
I rush outside. I should tell Marcus but he's acting as
though he's forgiven me. I don't want to make him mad
again.

For the rest of day, as we look around the other sets,
I wait for someone to yell at me. But no one mentions it
and I begin to wonder whether there was anyone there.
Perhaps it was just my imagination.

Marcus doesn't let me out of his sight and I have a
feeling I'm going to have to work hard to earn his trust
again. He literally hands me over to my stunt team back
at the bungalow, refusing to just drop me off.

'You need to keep an eye on this one,' he says, before
leaving.

'What did you do?' says Richie suspiciously.

'Nothing.'

'Hmm.'

I sit at the breakfast counter and he hands me
a thin booklet. 'Your script for tomorrow. It's pretty
straightforward.'

'We look forward to seeing what you can do,' says
Jenks, entering the room. 'The fourteen-year-old prodigy.'

No pressure then!

I open the booklet and flick through the pages. My heart plummets. Out of all the possible stunts in the world, why this?

CHAPTER

8

Even though it's four in the morning when Richie knocks on my bedroom door, I'm showered and dressed. I set my alarm to half three to make sure I woke up, but I needn't have bothered. I hardly slept, worrying about today.

'The tuk-tuks are waiting,' says Richie.

'The what?'

'Our taxis.'

I follow Richie outside and stare at the vehicles. They're three-wheeler open-sided cabins connected to mopeds. I clamber into the back with Richie, Jenks, and—unfortunately—Calum. I really hoped he wouldn't be with us today in case it all goes wrong.

'The tuk-tuk is the only way to travel,' says Richie.

As we speed through the streets, I decide it's official. Tuk-tuks are far more fun than limos. You feel the wind and hear the sounds. We head deeper into Hiva Hin, and despite it being the crack of dawn, Blake's fans line the roads. They hold banners with his name written next to giant love hearts and scream as we approach.

'You should pretend to be Blake,' says Richie. 'You look so alike.'

Keeping my face hidden, I lift my arm and wave. The girls erupt into even louder screams and suddenly I feel like a rock star. I could get used to this.

'If only they knew who they were really screaming for,' says Calum, sneering.

We pass through the barriers, leaving the fans far behind, and pull up outside a Thai market used by locals rather than tourists. Smells of spices, fruits, and fish fill the air, and crew members are everywhere, fiddling with lights and cameras. *What time did they get up?*

Today is a chase scene between Rio and the bad guys. Richie walks me through the route twice so I know exactly where I'm going. The market is massive with narrow pathways twisting between stalls packed tightly together. There are stands full of exotic fruits, herbs, and vegetables, lots I've never seen before. There's raw and barbecued meat, fish on ice, with some so strange, they look like they came from outer space rather than the sea.

There are plastic and cuddly toys piled high, along with railings upon railings of clothes.

'You think you can remember the route?' says Richie.

I nod. If only we were on foot for the real thing. He drops me off at a trailer for hair and make-up and the women look at me carefully.

'Wow, I can see why you're Blake's stunt double. We won't have to do that much to you,' says one of the make-up artists.

'I don't look much like him. It's just the hair.'

'Hey, it's a compliment,' she says, grinning.

'It really isn't.'

I can't look that much like Blake because it takes them an hour to turn me into Rio Dinoni. I'm taken to wardrobe next, where I'm put in jeans, T-shirt, and leather jacket. Plus Jenks insisted I wear knee, elbow, and back pads underneath Rio's normal clothing. It all feels like it's sticking to me and in a desperate attempt to cool down, I've already drunk two massive bottles of water.

'You look good,' says Richie, who has come to collect me. 'You ready?'

'Yeah,' I lie.

I step outside the trailer to find the horses already there. They're sleek and beautiful, like they could be racehorses. I try to keep my face as blank as possible. I don't want Richie picking up on my nerves.

'These horses are really well trained and they've been

46

through the market a good few times,' he says. 'Even more than you.'

'So they know where they're going?'

'Yeah. You just need to make sure yours goes at the right speed.'

I nod, clenching and unclenching my fists.

Richie's brow wrinkles. 'I checked your CV and it says you've had plenty of practice on a horse.'

'It does? I mean it does.' When I applied for my first job, I persuaded Mum to exaggerate and we never changed it.

'And you did ride at the stunt academy, didn't you?'

'Yeah. Honestly, Richie, there is nothing to worry about. I'll be fine.'

'OK,' he says, but I can tell he's doubting me. 'Just one more thing. I know you're used to the English style of riding, but you'll be riding western here. It's actually easier.'

We walk over to the brown horse and I stroke its muzzle. I like animals when I'm not having to gallop on them.

'You're beautiful,' I whisper.

'This is Apinya,' says the man holding the reins.

'You want to get up? Grab onto the pommel and pull yourself up,' says Richie, tapping the front of the saddle.

Come on Finn, be Rio Dinoni!

Acting as though I do this every day, I grab the pommel, put my foot in the stirrup and swing my leg over the horse.

Richie grins. 'Phew, you had me worried for a sec. You do know horses.'

I take hold of the reins and smile back. This feels OK. These horses are well trained. They know the route. I'll simply hold on and act like Rio.

'Do the smells not spook them?' I ask.

'As I said, they're well trained.'

'And I don't need a riding hat?'

'We're in Thailand. Not the UK.' Richie pats the horse. 'So you know the script? You're chasing one of the bad guys. He's got the sapphire and is trying to escape with it.'

I nod. Then my chest tightens. Calum appears dressed like a Thai warrior. *He's* playing the baddie? He swings up onto the horse next to mine and the Assistant Director joins us.

'Finn, this is who you're chasing,' says the AD. 'I don't want you catching him up, but you need to remain close enough so that you stay in the same shot. We want tension as you both gallop around corners, but don't crash into any stalls or kick an Extra.'

'I'll go slow if you want?' says Calum.

I want to kick that smirk right off his face. 'No need. It'll be an effort not to overtake.'

'Ooh, fighting talk,' says Richie.

Two cameramen climb onto their dollies—metal contraptions on wheels that make it easy to keep the filming steady. Calum and I take our places and the Extras get into position too. Strider's chosen to use real stall owners and regular customers to complete the scene.

'Lights ready? Cameras ready? Sound ready? Take one,' calls the AD through a megaphone.

I half expect Apinya to bolt but his ears prick up and that's it.

Richie lifts up his arm. 'Three, two, one, action!' he says, slicing it down.

Calum kicks his legs and gallops into the market. I kick my legs too and thank God the horse moves. Holding the reins in one hand, I grip the pommel with the other, and as we hurtle inside, I bounce up and down, slapping the saddle with my bum. This can't look good and so I try straightening my legs. It works a little.

Galloping through the stalls, I don't have to use the reins. Apinya knows what he's doing—just following the horse in front—but I feel like a passenger, not a rider. And Calum's getting away. I kick my legs harder and we burst forward. Heart pounding, I cling on, as we twist left and right. My foot knocks into a pile of bananas but luckily my horse keeps going. Why do the pathways have to be so narrow? Couldn't we have chased him through a field or at least a road?

Calum loops left past a flower stall and I charge after him. Then we turn a corner and something falls off one of the shelves right in front of my horse. Apinya rears onto his hind legs, flinging me backwards. I hurtle through the air, crashing into the worst smell ever. Ice falls over me and I lie still. I move my body, almost crying with relief that nothing's broken. Then I look around to discover I'm lying in fish guts. Out of all the possible stalls, I crashed into the one selling squid.

The crew rush towards me and burst out laughing. I don't believe it. Marcus, Blake, Jenks and Strider are with them too. Anyone else want to witness my humiliation? Someone grabs Apinya, who doesn't seem at all bothered now.

'That's one for the blooper roll,' says Richie, holding out his arm. 'Are you hurt?'

I shake my head. Even though I'm covered in ice, my face and neck feel so hot and I know I'm bright red as Richie pulls me up.

'Sorry,' I mutter.

'Whatever for? I've never laughed so much in my life,' says Richie, grinning at me. 'We've been watching it on the camera screens.'

'Something spooked my horse,' I say.

He raises an eyebrow.

'Something spooked Apinya. Something dropped in front of him.' I look around the floor but can't see a thing.

'Should we do it again?' says Jenks, sounding uneasy.

'Actually, why doesn't Blake do it himself?' says Marcus, suddenly.

'What?' Blake and I say at the same time and everyone turns to look at Saunders Senior.

'He's been wanting to do more stunts for a while now. I can give him permission—he's my son. He's very

50

experienced. He's been on horses since he was about three.'

Of course he has!

Jenks looks thoughtful. 'If he's that experienced, he won't bounce about on the back.'

'I bounced?'

'Like you were on a trampoline,' says Richie and everyone laughs again.

Except Strider and the AD. Neither looks pleased.

'What if Blake gets hurt?' says the director in his Californian drawl.

'Yeah, what if I get hurt?'

'You won't,' says Marcus. 'And what's the worst that can happen? You end up stinking of fish, like Finn.'

Oh great, I'm the worst that can happen!

Blake straightens his back and says, 'All right, I'll give it a go.'

'Yes!' His dad punches the air and everyone makes their way back to the other end of the market.

Watching them, my body grows cold. Is this why Marcus wanted to be in the film? He knew I wouldn't be good enough and he'd be able to persuade Blake to do his own stunts.

Feeling completely useless, I try to catch up.

CHAPTER 9

The cameras aren't filming. They just want to make sure Blake can ride. He swings onto Apinya like a professional cowboy. I'm surprised he didn't leapfrog. He kicks his legs and the horse begins to canter. Using the reins in one hand, he pulls Apinya around, as if he's starring in a western.

'He's a natural,' says Jenks.

'Way to go, Blake!' shouts Marcus.

Twenty minutes later, Blake's wearing padding under his clothes and they're filming. My jaw hurts, I've been clenching it so tightly. Standing behind the director with the others, I stare at the screen, watching Blake navigate the narrow pathways. He's never looked more like Rio than he does right now.

Richie turns to me. 'Finn, you might want to wash. You stink and you're making me sick.'

That gives me the perfect opportunity not to watch. I head to make-up's trailer where I know there's a sink.

'You're going to stink out my trailer,' says one of the make-up artists, but she lets me in. 'Don't expect me to stay though. I hate fish.'

As soon as she leaves, I look in the mirror. Someone could have told me that I have squid in my hair. Pulling it out, it squidges and slimes through my fingers. Urgh. I dump it in the bin, then wash my hands and face, and pluck the fish guts off my clothes. They're still covered in blood and squid juices. I'll go to wardrobe and find my own T-shirt but I need the toilet first. Heading to the loos, I glance at the market. I'm near a different entrance full of stalls filled with plastic and cuddly toys. Then something black moves in the shadows, leaping over the teddies.

What the—?

It's about the size of a cat but on two legs. It scurries across games, action figures, fluffy animals. It leaps right in front of the face of an Extra, but the man working the stall doesn't react at all. Something about the creature makes me uneasy, and before I know it, I'm running over to the market. The animal darts deeper into the stalls, disappearing from view. I try to find it, twisting left and right, but it's gone.

Then I hear the sound of hooves. They grow louder, which means the horses are coming this way. My stomach drops. I can't be found here. I'll be on film and they'll have to reshoot the scene. Looking around frantically, I scramble under a nearby table. Hiding amongst puzzles and cuddly toys, I peer out just in time to see Calum gallop past, chased by Blake. Suddenly a teddy flies through the air, right in front of Blake's horse. Apinya rears, but somehow Blake manages to hold on. He spins the horse around, bringing Apinya to a stop. Whoa! That looked impressive.

'Cut!' shouts the AD over the megaphone.

'Blake, are you all right?' shouts Marcus, running towards his son.

Natasha follows closely behind, her face contorted in fury. *When did she get here?*

'My son could have been killed!' she shouts. 'What was he doing on that horse?'

'You know he's a competent rider,' says Marcus.

'But not in a Thai market stall,' says Natasha, looking more and more angry. 'Where's Finn? Shouldn't he be on that horse, otherwise what's the point of him even being here?'

My mouth dries. That's a very good question.

Then I hear clapping and the director strides around the corner, a beam stretching across his face. 'Blake, you were marvellous. A true Rio.'

'He's not doing it again,' hisses Natasha. 'I don't care how many takes you want.'

'He doesn't have to. That footage was spectacular.'

I lower my head and wait until they all disappear, before peering out of the stall. The place is empty. Creeping out from under the table, I search for the toy on the ground but someone must have picked it up. I look towards the top of the stall where both teddies fell. Or were they thrown? Two toys falling in the same place just as a horse appears seems too much of a coincidence. But there doesn't seem to be anything out of the ordinary and so I head back to the trailers. My stunt team surrounds Blake, and they're all telling him how great he is. Do I have to witness that? It's not as if anyone is missing me.

Keeping to the shadows, I head out of the filming zone. It took us ten minutes to get here by tuk-tuk, so it will be longer on foot. It takes an hour. Arriving at the security gate, I half expect the guards to not let me through, but they get up from their seats in the hut, bow their heads and usher me past. Hopefully they recognize me, rather than just letting anyone in. With my head down, I walk past the bungalows. Then stop suddenly. An elephant stands in one of the front gardens, pulling out plants, munching happily.

Is this normal in Thailand? I look around but there doesn't seem to be anyone else here, human or animal.

I step closer to the giant beast. 'Where have you come from? Are you lost?'

'Are you expecting her to reply?' says a voice with a beautiful Thai lilt.

Startled, I turn around to see a girl step out from behind a tree. She's about my age, has jet-black hair, is covered in mud and carrying a basket.

'I thought she might tell me her address,' I say with a smile.

The girl doesn't smile back. She pulls out a banana from the basket and the elephant walks towards her. I jump out of the way.

'Is she yours?' I ask, as the elephant scoops up the banana in her trunk before dropping it in her mouth.

'Sort of. We own a sanctuary, not far from here. We look after rescued elephants.'

'That's cool.'

For a second, the girl's face softens. 'It is the best job in the world . . . unless they decide to escape.' She pats the elephant's neck, which seems intent on grabbing more fruit. The girl pulls the basket out of the way and the elephant's trunk snuffles around her. 'What are you doing here?' she asks.

'I'm part of the film crew. I work with Blake Saunders.'

I wait for her to swoon, gasp, ask for his autograph.

'Who?' she says.

Has she been living under a rock for the past few years? 'He plays Rio Dinoni?'

'Ah!' she says, nodding. 'They are using our elephants in the film.' Then her nose wrinkles. 'I smell fish.'

I feel my face redden, when the elephant turns and lumbers towards me. She lifts up her trunk and opens her mouth. I'm about to step away when the girl looks at me strangely.

'She wants you to stroke her tongue,' she says.

'What?'

'She wants you to stroke her tongue,' she repeats, as if this is the most natural thing in the world. 'She does not normally do that with strangers. She must like you.'

'She won't bite me?'

'Elephants do not bite. If they do not like you, they hit you with their trunk or trample you.'

'Good to know! But she definitely likes me?'

'Yes.'

I reach under the elephant's trunk and pause. This has got to be one of the strangest things I've ever done. I really hope this isn't a wind-up and that elephants don't bite. I stretch out my arm a little further and feel her tongue on my fingers. Whoa—it's soft and slimy. Everything seems to be slimy today. But stroking her tongue is really calming.

'You can stop now,' says the girl.

Part of me wants to ignore her, but perhaps the elephant wants me to stop too. I take my hand away.

'So. If your elephants are going to be in the film, I guess they're, like, actors too?' I say with a laugh.

The girl pulls a face. 'I wish they were not,' she snaps, and without a second glance in my direction, she walks away, waving the basket.

The elephant follows her. They disappear from view and when I realize they aren't coming back, I start heading to the bungalow again. A couple of streets away, I hear a beep. A tuk-tuk pulls up beside me, and Jenks leans out of the back.

'Get in,' he hisses, his face bright red.

I jump inside and the tuk-tuk starts again.

'What do you think you're doing?' says Jenks.

'Walking home.'

'Without your guardian? Without telling anyone?' He takes deep breaths and I think he might explode. 'Do you realize everyone's out looking for you?'

'Richie?'

He nods. 'And Strider and the Saunders.'

Oh God. I drop my head into my hands.

'Even if you are not performing, you stay and support your stunt team,' says Jenks.

'Blake isn't in my stunt team,' I say, the words slipping out before I can stop them.

'Oh I see. You were jealous.'

'No!'

'You were jealous and you thought you'd walk away, forgetting about the rest of us. Forgetting that you are in a foreign country and anything could happen to you. And who'd be responsible? Me.' He takes more deep breaths. 'As soon as we get back, I want you to go to your room.'

'What?'

'You heard me. I don't want to see your face for the rest of the day.'

'So you're sending me to my room?'

'Yep, you're grounded. And from now on, I don't want you going anywhere without a member of your stunt team present. Do I make myself clear?'

'Yes,' I mumble.

He rubs his forehead. 'Blimey, I feel like a dad not a boss. And you're aging me. I think I've got even more grey hair.'

'Is that possible?' I say, and Jenks throws me such an angry look, my mouth clamps shut.

The tuk-tuk comes to a halt beside our bungalow and I swing out of it. I kind of wish I'd been fired now instead of being treated like a baby.

Calum's going to love this.

CHAPTER 10

'Are you all right, Finn?' says Calum through my bedroom door. 'Or do you need a nappy change?'

Every muscle in my body tenses, before I turn over in bed and bang my elbow. *Oh, fabulous!* I bet criminals in prison have more room than this. Stuck in a box for hours is not exactly what I had in mind when I came to Thailand. In all honesty, it's not my room that's put me in this foul mood. I can't believe how much Blake showed me up earlier. He was great and I was so ridiculously rubbish.

There's a bang on my door. 'Finn, we're going to dinner,' calls Lucy.

'I'm not hungry.'

'Come on. You've got to eat. You need your strength for tomorrow.'

'He is such a child,' I hear Calum say, and my jaw clenches.

I can't let him be right and so I open the door, grateful that Calum's already walking away.

'We're going to the Thai Orchid,' says Lucy.

'Is Jenks still mad?'

'He'll get over it, but you won't see him anyway. He's on location, working out the stunt for tomorrow.' She leans towards me and lowers her voice. 'Listen, the others are going to make fun of you. They're going to make you squirm. But if you take it, and laugh along, it will be over soon.'

'How do you know?'

'You're not the only one who's messed up on a shoot.'

'What happened?'

'Oh no. I'm never telling you that.'

Ten minutes later, I'm walking into the restaurant with Lucy. The room erupts into cheers, the loudest coming from my stunt team.

'Watch out for the squid,' yells a cameraman I recognize.

Great—everyone knows!

I have no other option and it worked back at the academy. I take a bow and the room cheers even more.

'Well done,' whispers Lucy.

I grab a bowl and head over to the food, piling my bowl high with beef, vegetables, and noodles, staying well clear of the seafood. I don't think I'll ever be able to eat that again.

'Finn,' says Richie sharply, 'sit yourself down and eat your dinner.'

'And make sure you eat everything up or you will not get dessert,' adds Tom.

'Do we need to feed him?' says Calum with a malicious laugh.

I glance at Lucy who nods. 'Where's my bib?' I ask. 'I can't eat without my bib.'

They laugh and Richie even claps his hands. Calum looks disappointed.

They spend the entire meal ribbing me, but like Lucy suggested, I take it. I mock myself, and slowly but surely the conversation changes.

'Did you film any other scenes?' I ask.

Lucy shakes her head. 'Tom and I were supposed to do this mountain shoot but the lighting wouldn't work.'

'It was a nightmare. I was strapped to the gib and we had to stop. All that effort for nothing.' Tom leans back in his chair. 'People are saying this film is cursed.'

'What people?' says Richie.

'Locals and some of the film crew who come from Bangkok. Cameras, booms, and now that gib haven't been working. Plus the Wall of Death has to be fixed.'

'What's wrong with the Wall of Death?' I ask.

Tom grabs a prawn cracker. 'It's got this massive groove running around the middle. No one knows how it got there.'

'A groove?' I whisper.

It wasn't there yesterday and suddenly I remember the shadow on the balcony. Perhaps I wasn't hiding from him. He was hiding from me. And what about the toys spooking the horses?

Richie chuckles. 'The pair of you look so worried. Don't tell me you believe in curses? You'll tell me you believe in fairy tales next. We've hit a bit of bad luck, that's all.'

'The film's not going to be shut down, is it?' I burst out.

'Oh, man, is that what you're worried about? Cos that ain't going to happen. All movies have hiccups,' says Richie.

'I hope you're right,' says Tom, pushing his half-eaten plate away.

So do I!

Lucy, Tom, and—thankfully—Calum leave early, not bothering with dessert. Richie and I help ourselves to the sticky rice cooked in coconut milk. I could eat this forever.

'I wanted to have a little word with you in private,' says Richie. 'I'm thinking you haven't had that much experience on a horse. Calum hinted at that too.'

The little squealer!

'Is it true?'

Is there any point in lying? After all, Richie saw me on the horse. 'Yeah,' I admit. 'It was only the third time I rode. We couldn't afford lessons when I was younger.'

'I get that. They're expensive.' His voice becomes gentle. 'The thing is, Finn, I have to be able to trust you and you have to be able to trust me. That's how a stunt team works. If you've not done something before, tell me. I'm not going to be cross. You're only young. No one will think less of you. When you saw the script last night, you should have said.'

'I wanted to impress you.'

'You have impressed me. You're a fourteen-year-old stunt double.'

'I haven't impressed Strider.'

'Not yet, but you will. Now let's forget about today. Have you ever done free running?' He looks at me searchingly.

'Yes,' I say quickly.

'Truthfully?'

'Yes.'

'Then tomorrow is your lucky day. We'll go through the script when we get back. But. If there is anything you are worried about, and I mean anything, tell me.'

'I will.'

'Good. And Finn, if that really was the third time you've ever been on a horse, then you were pretty awesome.'

CHAPTER 11

Time to prove myself. I have to be better than I was yesterday.

I'm back in Rio gear, complete with padding, ready to start filming. I tried to get away without wearing it—arguing I don't need it and outside it's so hot—but Jenks insisted. Again.

Blake and I are in the lobby of a luxurious hotel. Everywhere I look, there are marble pillars, crystal chandeliers, mirrored walls, and stone sculptures of strange creatures. Five galleried landings look down on us. Plus the film crew are going crazy setting everything up. Cameras are being positioned throughout the hotel, ready to catch our every move.

'How are you feeling after yesterday?' says Blake.

'All right.'

'Really? I thought you'd be a little more—'

'Embarrassed?'

'Mortified,' he says with a grin, 'because you were so awful and I was unbelievably brilliant.'

'Oh yeah? Well, as you're so unbelievably brilliant, you can do today's stunts if you want. You don't mind leaping off a balcony, do you?'

Blake's eyes widen and he looks around. 'Don't say that out loud. Dad might make me.'

'Make you do what?' says Jenks, coming towards us.

'Nothing,' says Blake quickly.

I stand up straight as if Jenks is a military officer, all the while trying to read his expression. Is he still mad at me? Then I spot Strider behind him and I stand even taller. I haven't actually spoken to the director yet and the only thing he's seen me do—is crash.

'I'm sorry about yesterday,' I blurt out.

'Yesterday's news,' says Jenks, waving his hand, brushing my words away. 'We've moved on.'

'Just before we move on,' says Strider, lifting his finger into the air, 'I really should thank you.'

'Thank me?'

'You've been great publicity. Someone uploaded the clip to YouTube and it's had millions of hits.'

'Really?' My insides squirm. Please say no one at home saw it. 'Is that allowed? I thought films had to be secretive and no one's supposed to know I do stunts or that I'm Blake's stunt double.'

'Well, as the secret's out, it's out. Nothing we can do about it now. And we were never going to use that footage anyway so it's OK. But we don't want anything else getting out. So let's try to be a bit more professional today.'

'You've practised the route with Richie?' says Jenks.

'Three times.'

'Great.' Then Jenks scans the area. 'Where is Richie? He's supposed to be with you.'

I point to Richie who's sitting down with a cowboy hat pulled low on his head. I think he's trying to catch some sleep. Strider claps his hands and Richie leaps to attention.

'OK, guys, we're ready to start!' yells Strider.

Extras appear en masse, dressed like staff or tourists. They fill the lobby and I recognize one of them. The girl with the elephant, except now she's dressed like a smart tourist. I catch her eye and lift my hand in a feeble wave. She scowls and turns away.

'Still a hit with the girls,' whispers Blake, nudging me.

Ten minutes later, the cameras are rolling. I watch Rio try to rent a room from the receptionist. She looks at his passport uncertainly.

'Are your parents here?' she asks.

'My parents are in prison,' says Rio.

The woman's eyes widen and Rio taps his fingers on the desk. Then he looks left and his face fills with fear.

'Never mind,' he says, snatching his passport from the receptionist.

He starts to run.

'And, cut!'

Strider claps his hands. 'Blake, that was awesome. Finn, on your marker.'

I walk to the spot where Rio stopped, a few metres away from the reception desk, and replicate his running pose.

'I want urgency and tension. Rio knows too much and the secret sect will do anything to keep him quiet,' says Strider. 'Tom and Calum will be chasing you, but they're under strict instructions not to catch you up. So don't kill yourself trying to be fast.'

He thinks I'm going to be rubbish, like I was on the horse. I take a deep breath. I have to show him.

As soon as Strider walks out of the shot, someone booms, 'Cameras ready? Lights ready? Sound ready? Scene 103, Take one.'

I look at Jenks.

'Three, two, one, action.' His hand lowers.

I start to run.

Pumping my arms like Blake, I race through the lobby, dodging families and couples. Glancing over my shoulder, I see Tom lagging behind but Calum's catching up. He's not supposed to do that. I put on a sudden burst, leapfrogging over a counter, my feet narrowly missing a tour guide. I head straight for the spiral staircase, bounding up the steps two at a time. Hurtling along the landing, I briefly look back again. *You're kidding?* Calum's closing the gap. Then I knock straight into a woman dragging a suitcase.

'Sorry!' I shout.

That's not meant to happen but hopefully it will make it look more realistic. Spotting the actor opening a door, I barge past her into the suite.

'Hey!' she shouts.

I run past her open-mouthed children sitting on the sofa and rush into the second room. Springing off a double bed, my feet bounce off the walls, as I slide open the glass door. Without touching the ground, I swing onto the balcony. Then pause for a second. This is why I have padding. I leap three metres to the grass below. Landing, knees bent, I look back up to see Calum grabbing the railings. He's supposed to be further back. Is he trying to make me look rubbish?

Racing as fast as I can, I head for the high wall. My right foot hits it about waist height and I drive hard through my leg, pushing myself upwards. I grab the peak with both hands and scramble to the top. Standing on the narrow ledge, I'm about to jump down. But just like the script says, I see more enemies running towards me. I can't go forward. I glance back—Calum's nearly on me now. My only option is to go along the narrow ledge. Arms outstretched like a tightrope walker, I run as fast as I dare.

My heart pounds. I can't slip. Looking over my shoulder, I see Calum on the wall too . . . but he's a lot slower. I can outrun him here. The wall bends around. I snake along to the spot where I jump to safety. I roll on the ground as I land, grabbing onto my leg, as if hurt. Then I scramble back to my feet and head straight for the long stone pond filled with koi fish. It's about a foot off the ground but narrow enough to jump across. That's when I see it.

Silver wire glinting in the light, stretching about two feet above the pond. And I hear a cackle. What the—? Suddenly I realize I'm slowing down. Strider won't be pleased. I speed up again and leap over the wire, scaling the pond. Then I pound the ground as fast as I can.

Seven steps away, I think of Calum. Will he see the wire?

CHAPTER 12

There's a massive shriek and a splash.

I glance over my shoulder. Calum scrabbles about in the pond, but I have to keep going for the film. I look forward again, turn a corner then hear the word: 'Cut.'

I sprint back. 'Are you OK, Calum?'

He stands in the centre, seaweed hanging from his hair, blood dripping down his leg.

'You did this!' he shouts, pointing at me.

'What?'

'You tripped me. You put something there to make me fall.'

'What are you talking about?' says a cameraman, coming towards us.

71

'I saw him leap higher. He must have known something was there. My ankle hit something, made me trip.'

'But there was something there,' I say. 'There was a wire across the pond.' But when I look down, it's gone. 'Could someone have moved it?'

We peer around. There are so many people here, anyone could have done it, although how without us seeing is another question.

'Let me take another look on playback,' says the cameraman, and we huddle around the screen on the camera watching Calum jump. Nothing.

'But he felt it and I saw it. Is it possible the camera didn't pick it up?'

'Pretty unlikely.' The cameraman zooms in on the pond and there's no flash of silver.

'This doesn't make sense,' I whisper. The wire has gone, just like the toys in the market. Is Tom right? Could this film be cursed?

We hear a honk and a golf cart veers into view. Strider, Jenks, and Richie leap out.

'That was amazing!' shouts Strider. 'We were watching on the screen and it felt so real. The urgency, the panic. Finn, you are some free runner. I'm impressed.'

In spite of everything, I smile.

'And you Calum, you're good too. That trip was inspired. Such a great idea when you saw you were too close.'

Calum opens his mouth, then shuts it again.

'Now can you do it again? We need to do two more takes at least.'

Both Calum and I nod, but Strider's eyes fall to his bleeding leg. 'Walk for me,' he says.

Calum moves forward and I know he's trying really hard to hide his limp. He fails.

'Richie, you'll have to take his place,' says Strider. 'I want you to fall into the pond too.'

'Great,' says Richie with a grin. 'I love free running.'

Calum glares at me and I know I've given him a reason to hate me even more.

By the time we've filmed two more takes I am utterly exhausted. My legs and arms scream in agony. Richie is just as good, if not better than Calum, and I think Strider told him to keep the pressure on, possibly chase me even faster.

*

That night, I sink my aching body into bed desperate for sleep when my phone pings. It's a message from Sam.

OMG! Ur not at ballet camp. Ur a stuntman + never told me.

U can't ride a horse and probably stink of fish.

Enough of the boring news. I'm taking Mel 2 the cinema.

I burst out laughing, thinking of Sam with Mel. How on earth did he manage that? Then bubbles of excitement start welling up in my chest. Sam knows I'm a stuntman, which means everyone else back home will too. I wish I could see Ollie's face.

And I think about ringing Sam. I could tell him all about it—how I actually did well today; perhaps even mention how the film may be cursed. He'd love that. Then I remember my secrecy contract and how Sam is the world's worst secret-keeper.

CHAPTER
13

My legs still ache when we get up early the next morning. Do movie people not believe in lie-ins? According to Richie, we're going to an unspoilt part of Thailand. We're filming an important scene where Rio's trying to prove himself to the Thai sect, hoping to discover the location of the jewel. I read the script and it should be an easy shoot, as long as I don't see a wire or anything else that vanishes mysteriously. I want to—no, I have to—be just as good as yesterday.

Travelling in tuk-tuks, we head to the rainforest and the view is spectacular—mountains covered in lush green trees and ferns.

'That's Monkey Mountain,' says Richie, pointing to the right.

'Why's it called that?'

He looks at me as if I'm stupid. 'Because it's covered in vicious monkeys. Hundreds if not thousands of them live there. People don't visit any more because the monkeys kept attacking them.'

'Nice!'

'Tourists used to come from all over to see and feed the monkeys. And botanists used to come here too because of the rare parrot flower. It's supposed to look like exactly like the bird.'

'How do you know all this stuff?'

'I've been reading,' he says, holding up a travel guide.

We leave Monkey Mountain far behind and eventually break left into a track cut through the forest. Suddenly I feel uneasy. Is this supposed to be the unspoilt part? It's filled with cameras, cranes, lighting, and people trampling the ground. When we were in Papua New Guinea, we heard birds and strange creatures screeching. Now I hear machinery and human voices.

I spend an hour in hair, make-up, and wardrobe, and come out looking like Rio, except this time I'm not wearing his usual action hero gear. I'm dressed like an ancient Thai warrior with silk trousers and an armoured chest plate. I'm also wearing a jerk vest underneath—it looks a bit like a deflated lifejacket covered in hooks. I tried saying it wasn't necessary, but Jenks was having none of it.

I meet Blake outside, who's dressed identically, although I doubt he's wearing the jerk vest. We follow Jenks and Richie deeper into the jungle.

'Have you heard about all the stuff going wrong with this film?' whispers Blake.

'Yeah. It's not good, is it?'

'Mum's going mad. She keeps worrying that something bad will happen to me. I think she's trying to persuade Dad to pull us out.'

My heart stops. 'You're not going to, are you?'

'No chance. I can cope with anything. I am Rio Dinoni—Aargh—get this spider off me!' He frantically brushes the cobweb off his face.

I could possibly help if I wasn't laughing so much. The tiniest spider falls to the ground.

'Yeah, you're a real Rio,' I say.

'It could have been poisonous.'

OK, maybe he has a point.

We stop at the bottom of a massive tree that must have been here for hundreds of years. It's about thirty metres high, with vines dangling from tall branches. We crane our necks.

'You have to climb one of those vines?' says Blake.

'To the very top.' I'm beginning to feel grateful for the jerk vest. I'd no idea it was going to be this high.

'You better make me look good,' he says. 'I want streamline climbing.'

'As good as you looked fighting off that vicious spider? You Thai warrior, you!'

Blake grins. 'No one could look that good.'

I hear feet crunching the undergrowth and turn to see Calum.

'It's a shame we can't race for real,' he says.

It's a shame your leg's better. I'd much rather do this scene with Richie. 'You think you could beat me?' I say.

He smiles smugly.

We stand to the side and watch Blake nail his scene. He does three takes, but it was obvious the first one was fine. Jenks clips wires to the hooks on my vest, connecting me to a nearby crane in case I fall, and Richie hands me a pair of thick black military gloves.

'We want you to have a bit of a practice before we start filming,' says Jenks. 'Just have a go at climbing. Go about a quarter of the way up, but take it easy; conserve your energy.'

Calum and I walk to the base of our vines. They're about a metre apart from each other.

'Three, two, one, go!' says Richie.

I grab the vine as high as I can and pull myself up. Squeezing my boots together, I reach for a higher grip. One hand at a time, I yank upwards, as quickly as possible. Argh, Calum is quicker. He's at least half a person ahead of me.

'OK, that's enough. You both can do it,' yells Richie.

Sliding back down, the vine slips between my palms.

'I was saving myself,' I say, landing at the bottom.

'So was I,' says Calum.

I hope he's lying too.

Jenks rolls his eyes. 'You looked good, both of you. But Calum, remember Finn has to be faster than you. If it looks like you're getting to the top first, slow down, otherwise you'll be doing it again.'

'We're only doing one take?' I say hopefully.

'It's up to Strider, but if you do well, who knows?' He pauses. 'And please don't try to go too fast at the beginning. You've got a long way to go. So don't really race.'

Jenks moves out of the shot and the cameras start rolling. I watch Richie.

'Three, two, one, action,' he says, his arm slicing down.

I grasp the vine, and, using my hands and feet, pull myself up. I know Jenks said not to go too fast, but this *is* supposed to look like a race. I yank higher and quicker, but soon my arms and legs begin to burn. Glimpsing down, I can't believe it. I'm only halfway. Calum's not that far behind and he sneers up at me. I pull harder again, my palms sweating in the gloves and my back dripping. Even though I must be moving, the top doesn't seem to be getting any nearer. I feel myself slowing down. *Come on, Finn, you're Rio, an action hero.* Somehow I keep climbing ... up and up. Soon my muscles scream for me to stop. Looking down again, Calum's face is glowing red. Obviously he's not finding it that easy now either. We should have thought of some invisible sign to let us both take a breather.

Suddenly I hear a cackle in my ear, like the laughter I heard at the pond but much closer. And something drops on my back. *What the—?* Clinging onto the vine with one hand, I reach my other arm around to pull it off. My fingers grasp fur.

'What is it?' I yelp.

'Shut up and keep going,' snarls Calum.

Can't he see there's a *thing* on my back? Is he not looking up at me? I try to yank the creature off when I hear clicks. Whisking my head around, I watch in horror as the wires from my jerk vest fall to the ground. I glance at Calum, but he's facing the other way. I swear loudly. Nothing can save me if I fall. I'm about twenty metres off the ground clinging on by one hand. Releasing the fur, I grab onto the vine again. The creature scrambles over my head, its long tail brushing my face. Is that a monkey? Why and how did he unclip me?

It scales the rest of my vine, reaching the branch we're trying to get to. Then its tail curls around the bough and it dangles down, bearing its teeth in an evil grin. Since when do monkeys have glowing amber eyes? Somewhere in the back of my mind I'm sure I've seen it before ...

'Calum,' I hiss. 'Calum, can you see this?'

'See what?' he snaps, still not looking up. 'Keep climbing or we'll have to do it again.'

The monkey stretches out its arms and long dagger-like claws sprout from its hands. *What? How?* Then I watch in frozen horror as it swipes its claws against the top of my vine.

CHAPTER 14

Threads of vine rip away. It's not going to hold my weight much longer. Even though every fibre in my body screams at me to keep away from such a thing, I have to stop the monkey or I'll plummet to the ground. Climbing even faster, I grow closer, but there's no way I'll make it in time. With no other choice, I take a deep breath and stretch out my arm. I throw myself across the gap, grabbing Calum's vine in my hands. Wrapping my legs around it, my foot narrowly misses his head.

'What are you doing?' he shrieks, but I can't even speak.

I just cling on, before my old vine tumbles to the ground.

Calum swears. Then shouts, 'Keep going. I'm not sure this will hold us.'

Feeling as though my arms are ripping from their sockets, I keep climbing. The creature scuttles along the branch until it's directly above us, its claws dangerously close to the vine. *Not this one too!* My adrenalin spikes and I yank myself up the rest of the plant. I try to grab the hairy creature, but it bounds out of reach. With its claws reducing to their normal size, it darts through the top of the trees. I drag my body onto the branch, and while keeping my hands and feet connected to the wood, I scramble to the trunk. Calum pulls himself up too.

'What was that thing?' I whisper, hugging the tree.

'What thing?'

How could he have missed it? 'That thing with glowing eyes and claws.'

Calum looks at me as if I'm completely mad. 'Are you hallucinating?'

Am I hallucinating? But if I am, what the hell unhooked my wires?

'Is the air up here getting to you?' he adds.

I know I shouldn't, but I peer down. Whoa! We're high, and I'm stranded up here. My body grows hot, my head feels dizzy. Then to my utter relief, a crane appears with a box at the top. I scrabble into it and Calum follows me inside. A minute later, we're back on the ground, with Strider and Jenks rushing towards us.

'I've watched the playback. That was amazing,' says the director. 'Finn, your leap was inspired.'

'Not that inspired,' I mutter. Then, louder, I say, 'I had to. My vine was torn off by a black monkey.'

Strider and Jenks stare at me.

'You think a monkey broke your vine?' says Jenks finally.

Calum snorts. 'There was nothing there. He was hallucinating because of the height. The vine broke because Finn obviously weighs more than he looks. We should stop feeding him pies.'

Jenks and Strider look at each other before back at me. 'Were you hallucinating?' asks the director.

'I did feel dizzy up there.'

'Well, that will be it, then. You had me worried for a minute. We don't want to lose our best stunt double.'

Calum scowls.

'Are you OK now?' says Jenks, watching me carefully.

Best stunt double? 'I'm fine. Just tell me we don't have to film that stunt again. I don't think I have the strength to go back up.'

'That take was perfect,' says Strider.

Phew!

Calum stretches out his arms, pumping his biceps. 'I wouldn't mind doing it again.'

Yeah, right!

'Let me unhook you both,' says Jenks. Then he stares at my vest in horror. 'Where are your wires?'

'They were—' *unclipped by a freaky monkey with glowing eyes and sprouting claws.* I think of their faces seconds earlier. 'They fell off.'

'So you were up there with no back-up? You made that jump with no—' His words drop away.

Even Calum looks surprised.

Strider beams. 'That is why it was so impressive. The tension, the fear on your face. I'll have to get Blake to mirror it.'

'Where is Blake?' I ask.

'He left after his shoot. He was needed elsewhere,' says Strider.

Jenks looks at my vest again, his jaw clenching. 'What is going on with this film?' he mutters.

I wish I knew!

I traipse back through the undergrowth with my stunt team when I stop. Why didn't I ask to see the footage? That monkey-thing must be on it. But then Strider would have seen it, as well as the cameraman, and Richie. Surely someone would have said something, wouldn't they?

'Where is Richie?' I ask, looking around.

Jenks closes his eyes, before opening them again. 'There was an accident.'

'What?' My blood runs cold. 'Is he hurt?'

'Not Richie, but his friends. Dan and Will from lighting. They were rushed into hospital.'

'Are they all right?'

'I don't think so,' says Jenks, shaking his head slowly. 'They were on a moped going back to the bungalows, when it somersaulted through the air. People are talking about a wire across the road. Almost invisible.'

My blood doesn't just run cold. It turns to ice.

CHAPTER 15

As soon as we get back to the bungalow, I head to my room and grab my mobile. Pressing the Google app, I type 'black hairy monkey with glowing eyes' and hit *search*. Nothing happens. I stare at the top left of the screen. Argh—there's no coverage.

'Don't we have Internet?' I ask, rushing back into the lounge.

Jenks and Calum are helping themselves to some snacks, and Lucy and Tom are lying on the sofas watching TV.

'It only seems to work half the time,' says Lucy. 'The restaurant has it though.'

'You can use it when we go for dinner,' adds Jenks.

'When will that be?'

'About nine.'

I glance at my watch. Two hours away!

'Would any of you escort me there now? Or I can go on my own?'

'You're not allowed to go anywhere on your own and we're all busy,' says Jenks.

Doing what?

But to be honest I can't research this in front of them anyway. They'll ask me what I'm up to. I trudge back to my room, fall onto my bed and my heart stops. I know where I've seen that creature before. Then the window seems to wink at me. Within seconds I'm on my knees, trying the handle and pushing the glass to see if it will open. The pane pivots upwards.

'Jenks, I yell. 'Can I have a nap?'

'That's a good idea,' he shouts. 'We'll wake you up for dinner.'

'Do you need a bedtime story?' quips Calum.

I roll my eyes, before pushing the glass even harder. The gap isn't that big, but I manage to squeeze my body through it, flopping onto the grass on the other side. Not the most glamorous of moves, but it did the trick. Running across the back garden, I leap over next door's hedge. Keeping to the shadows and watching out for any film crew, I dart from tree to tree. Luckily no one's around and soon I slip onto the road where the restaurant is. Walking casually as if nothing's up, I peer through the window of the Thai Orchid. Please don't let any of Jenks's friends be in there.

Yes! It's almost empty.

I hurry through the door and grab a bowl, pretending I'm after food.

'Excuse me?' I say to the nearest woman working behind the counter. 'Do you know what that monkey thing is?' I point to the large painting of mythological creatures on the wall behind her.

She looks at it for a second before turning back around to face me. 'I am sorry. I do not recognize that creature. I can tell you about the lion though. He is—'

My heart sinks and I hardly hear her words.

'Are you asking about the Lingphi?' says a voice behind me. I turn to find a woman of about sixty pointing at the hairy monkey.

My blood starts pumping around my body. 'That— that's a Lingf—what?'

'A Lingphi.' She spells it out for me, then frowns. 'They are dreadful things. We should not have his picture in the restaurant.'

'What's so dreadful about them?'

'They—'

'Are not real,' says a third waitress joining us.

The old woman waves a spoon in the air. 'Of course they are real. They come from—'

'Finn!'

89

I almost jump out of my skin. Turning around, I see Marcus smiling at me.

'Sorry, I didn't mean to startle you.'

'You didn't,' I lie.

'I was heading home when I saw you through the window. You here for food?'

'Yeah. And the Internet.'

'Well, as great as the food is here,' he says, smiling at the ladies who all swoon, 'why don't you come to ours for something to eat? We're about to have dinner. We have Internet too.'

'That's all right.' I really want to talk to the waitresses some more.

'I am not taking no for an answer.'

Before I know it, his hands are on my shoulder and I'm being led out of the restaurant. I glance back at the picture and the old woman, but she seems to have forgotten I even exist. She's staring dreamy-eyed at Marcus.

'I can use the Internet at yours then?' I ask.

'Definitely.'

He steers me down the road and I check to see if anyone's watching. Even though I'm with *the* Marcus Saunders, I should have asked Jenks. Sneaking out probably wasn't my best idea. We turn into a road I've not been down before and I have to stop my jaw from dropping.

'Is this where you're staying?' I say, staring at the top

of the mansion peeking out from above the thick wall of flowering tropical trees.

'Nice, isn't it?' says Marcus. 'A home from home.'

'Blake must be pleased. It's at least five-star accommodation.'

'Hmm,' says Marcus.

He leads me past the perfectly manicured garden, complete with mermaid fountain, and opens the front door. A hotel-style lobby greets me. He undoes his shoes and I kick off mine.

'We have a visitor,' calls Marcus.

Natasha and Blake appear at the same time. Surprise flashes across Blake's face but then he grins. Natasha looks like she's eaten a lemon.

'He's come for dinner,' says Marcus.

'Does Ying know?' says Natasha.

'I'm sure she'll be fine with adding one more.' Marcus walks through a door to our left and we all follow.

I could be in a very posh restaurant. Three places are set with napkins in glasses, bowls on plates, and more cutlery than three people could possibly use. An elderly woman walks in, wearing a silk dress. She clasps her hands together and bows. The Saunders do the same and so I follow suit.

'Ying, would it be awfully difficult to add an extra person?' says Marcus.

'Of course not,' says the woman.

She smiles at me before disappearing through the

door she came from. Marcus grabs a chair from beside a wall and adds it to the table. Then he starts moving glasses and plates, creating a space. Blake and I help, while Natasha frowns. Ying returns with another place setting and at last we sit down. It did seem a bit of an effort so why was I invited? Was it to keep Blake entertained again?

'I saw the footage from yesterday with you running around the hotel, and your vine climb and leap today,' says Marcus. 'You were brilliant. A real action hero. A real Rio.'

'Thanks,' I say. *Would it be rude to ask to use the Internet now?*

'Blake, have you thought about taking up free running?' says Marcus.

'Erm, I—' he begins.

'Why would he want to?' says Natasha. 'That's why we have stunt doubles.'

'It was just a thought,' says Marcus, taking the napkin out of his glass and putting it on his lap. 'Make him a bit more tough.'

Blake looks down at the table and suddenly I wish I'd stayed at the restaurant.

Ying enters the room again, this time carrying a huge iron pot from which come the most delicious smells.

'Tom Yum soup,' she says, putting it down in the centre of the table. Ladling it into our bowls, she adds, 'A Thai speciality. Soup with spices, chicken, and prawns.'

Seafood? My stomach somersaults, but it smells so good and I'm hungry. I'm going to have to try it. I start devouring my bowl when I realize everyone is looking at me.

'It's like eating with the Simpsons,' says Natasha.

'It's nice to see a boy with a healthy appetite,' says Marcus. 'You enjoy it, son.'

Natasha gasps. *Am I not supposed to have a healthy appetite?* I grab my napkin and wipe my face. Whoops. Red soup is covering it. It must have been spattered all over my face. No one talks and I shift in my seat. Come on, someone say something.

'Blake, you were great on the horse the other day,' I say at last. 'I thought you were going to take my job. They wouldn't need me any more.'

'He was great,' says Marcus. 'But then he has had lessons for years.'

Blake keeps eating and doesn't look up.

'He shouldn't have even been on that horse,' mutters Natasha. Then in a louder voice she says, 'Did you hear about the moped accident today?'

Marcus nods.

'Do you know if they're OK?' I ask. 'I heard they went to hospital.'

'I'm waiting for a phone call.'

'People are saying the film is cursed,' says Natasha.

'That's because it is,' says Ying, entering the room again.

'Goodness, not you too,' says Marcus, his eyes

flickering between his wife and Ying. 'This film is not cursed.'

'Yes, it is.' Ying plucks the large bowl of soup off the table. 'When will you believe me? When someone actually dies?'

Natasha slams the table with both hands, making us all jump. 'We do not talk about death at the dinner table.'

Ying nods her head, but I can see she's desperate to say more, as she walks stiffly out of the room.

'Can I go to the toilet?' I blurt out.

'We don't mention toilet at the dinner table either. We say "bathroom",' says Natasha.

'Yes, of course you can,' says Marcus, glaring at his wife. 'It's down the corridor, second door on the right.'

I hurry out of the room and find the bathroom straight away. I almost laugh. It's twice the size of my room back at the bungalow. There's even an armchair. Falling into it, I pull out my mobile. *Yes!* I have Internet coverage. I type in *Lingphi* and three sites appear.

CHAPTER
16

Clicking on the first site, I read as quickly as I can. *The Lingphi is a demon in mythology said to carry out the biddings of others. Cackling as it performs its deeds, it's about two feet tall, and resembles a black hairy monkey with golden eyes and extendable claws. It is only visible to those who summoned it. People who can summon it are known as Lingphian.*

That's it! That's the creature. I heard it cackle and it's black and hairy, although I'd say its eyes are amber rather than gold. It explains why Calum didn't see it because he didn't summon it. But then . . . why can I?

More importantly, who the hell did? Because that creature isn't working alone. Someone else summoned it to put out trip wires and cut down vines. But why? Is it to stop the—

'Finn, are you all right?' calls Blake through the door.

'I'm—I'm fine. Just have a bit of a stomach ache.'

'Can't take the spicy food,' says Blake with a laugh.

'I guess.'

'My parents thought you might have drowned. I thought you might have made a bid for freedom. Escaped through the window.'

'I'll be out in a minute,' I say.

'I'll leave you to it then.'

As I hear him step away, I click on the second site and then the third. They say pretty much the same thing, although they call it a ghost monkey rather than a demon. I think I prefer that name. Standing up, I slide my phone back into my pocket. The words I've read are spinning around my head as I rejoin the Saunders in the dining room. Somehow I manage to eat the food on my plate and make polite conversation, although I'm not really sure what I'm saying. I want to be alone.

'What time is it?' says Marcus, once dinner is over.

'8.57,' says Natasha.

'What?' I jump up, my heart pounding.

'Are you Cinderella?' says Marcus. 'About to turn into a pumpkin?'

'I might be turned into one,' I mutter. Then in a louder voice I say, 'Thanks ever so much for having me. But I have to go.'

'Don't you want to use the Internet?'

'That's all right. Maybe another time.'

'OK,' says Marcus a little curiously. 'Blake, see him to the door.'

I follow Blake into the lobby.

'What's up? Why do you have to leave so quickly?'

'I didn't tell my stunt team I was coming. I snuck out.'

'So? Tell them you were with me. You'll be fine.'

'No, I won't. I've got to go now; I need to get in through my window before they fetch me for dinner.'

'You have to eat again?'

I don't answer as I'm already running. Hurtling through the back gardens, I leap over walls and charge through bushes. Dogs bark—some even howl—but thankfully they don't chase me. Reaching our back garden, I've no idea what time it is. I race across the lawn when I spot Calum looking out of his bedroom window. Noooooo! Maybe he hasn't seen me. I duck down, but when I glance back up, there's an evil grin plastered across his face. I am in so much trouble. He disappears from the window, no doubt getting Jenks.

I have seconds to get to my room. I run up the wall, grabbing onto my window frame. My toes scrabble at the stone as I try to heave myself in. My foot slips and I fall back down. Come on! I need to stop rushing. I hear someone knock on my door and call my name. They sound irritated. Backing away for a good run-up, I charge the wall again. This time I get a better grip and pull myself upwards.

The knocking gets louder, when the doorbell rings. The knocking stops. Have they gone to answer the door? Throwing myself inside, I land on my bed and try to catch my breath. Suddenly I hear lots of footsteps.

'We've been calling him for ages,' says Lucy.

'I bet he's not even in there,' says Calum, the glee in his voice detectable even through the door.

'Finn is a really deep sleeper,' says a voice I recognize. 'You don't know how many times I've had to literally slap him to wake him up.'

'Really?' says Lucy.

'Yeah. Let me try.' There's a massive bang on the door, then I hear Blake shout, 'Finn, wake up!'

I could hug him!

I stumble off my bed and open the door, rubbing my eyes as if the world is blurry.

'What? How?' says Calum. 'He wasn't in there.'

'I've been in here the whole time,' I say. 'Blake, what are you doing here?'

But Blake doesn't answer. He stares at my room. 'This is smaller than an aeroplane toilet.'

'It's fine,' I say. 'I just pretend I'm Harry Potter.'

'He had more room than you,' says Blake. 'Anyway, I came by to discuss tomorrow's stunt.'

'You know what it is?' I say.

'Yeah. I have the script. Your stunt's hard core. Dad's not even sure you should do it.'

'Do you know what I'll be doing?' says Calum.

'No,' says Blake. 'Why would I?'

Calum's face drops. 'No, of course you wouldn't.'

We hear the front door open again.

'I bet it's Tom,' says Lucy, and she and Calum return to the lounge.

As soon as they're out of sight, I say, 'Thank you so much.'

'You owe me big time. I ran all the way here,' whispers Blake.

Then I hear Lucy yelp, 'Richie, how are Will and Dan?'

Without waiting another second, Blake and I barge into the lounge. My stomach drops. Richie looks dreadful.

'Dan is fine. But Will—' Richie's voice cracks '—is in intensive care. They're not sure if he's going to live.'

'Oh God.' Lucy's hands fly to her cheeks.

Horror fills everyone's faces.

'Are the police involved because of the wire?' I ask.

'It's strange. It seems that Dan's the only one who saw it,' says Richie, flopping into the sofa. 'There were loads of people around and no one else saw a thing. If there was a wire, it seems to have disappeared as soon as they hit it.' He leans his head back. 'Tom's right. All the locals are talking about this film—saying it's cursed. Even the nurses think so.'

Ying's words come back to me. 'When will you believe me? When someone actually dies?'

But I think Ying and the nurses are wrong. This film's not cursed. I think someone summoned the Lingphi to sabotage it. The question is: who?

CHAPTER 17

I look around for a flash of black fur. I can't see the Lingphi, but it could be hiding anywhere, just waiting to leap out and cause trouble. My heart won't stop pounding. My palms are sweaty. It occurred to me last night that the sabotage seems to be getting worse. The demon started with bulbs breaking and stealing scaffolding but it's moved on to tearing down vines and setting wire traps across the road. Is whoever summoned it getting more desperate? What will they order the demon to do next?

We're in a massive warehouse close to one with the Wall of Death inside. *I really don't want to think about death!* The set designers have created the front of a luxury shopping mall, three storeys high, made almost entirely out of glass. It's similar to the mall near to where we're staying, but the owners didn't want us filming there. Having read the script, I don't blame them. We would wreck their shop.

I'm on the middle floor, amongst railings of expensive clothes, immediately behind the front panel of glass. I'm dressed in a dinner suit, the sort James Bond wears when he goes to a casino. I've got padding underneath, which isn't helping with the whole sweating thing. I scan the room for about the hundredth time.

'You look nervous,' says Richie. 'You sure you're OK with this stunt?'

'I'm fine.'

I squeeze my hands together. I have to concentrate on what I'm about to do and forget about the Lingphi. Peering through the glass, I see the crash mat below, as well as Jenks, Strider, the engineers, camera crew, and lighting setting up. It looks chaotic as they fiddle with the electronic gadgets. Apparently, after all that's been going on, they're checking everything at least three times, not leaving anything to chance.

'You've used an air ram before, right?' says Richie.

'At the academy.'

'Good.'

I tear my eyes away from the window to look at him. 'Have you heard any more about Dan and Will?'

'Yeah, Dan's out of hospital. He's only got a few scratches, so I think he's feeling a bit of a fraud. Will, on the other hand, is still in intensive care but at least he's stable.'

My heart starts pounding so loudly that I'm surprised Richie can't hear it. What if the Lingphi goes after me again? What if I end up in intensive care or worse? Or someone else does. I look around the film crew again. Whoever summoned that creature could be here right now.

'You sure you're OK?' says Richie.

Somehow I manage to utter the words, 'I've never been finer.'

And then I see it.

In the shadows, near a camera gib, two bright amber eyes shine out. They look straight at me and wink. My stomach drops. But I'm not going to show I'm scared.

'I'll be right back,' I say.

'Hey!' says Richie. 'We're about to start film—'

I don't wait to hear the rest. I run through the pretend boutique for the stairs at the back. Bounding down, three at a time, I hurtle into the room full of camera crew. Leaping over wires, I run straight for the corner.

'Watch it!' shouts a cameraman.

It seems as though the Lingphi was waiting for me. It winks again. As soon as I get close, it jumps onto a camera gib, scampering across the crane. I charge after it, when suddenly it turns 180 degrees. It springs right in front of me and I try to grab it, my fingers only grazing fur as it swoops by.

'What are you doing?' someone shouts.

Without answering, I chase the creature. I jump over a row of lights set low to the ground.

'You'll break something,' someone cries.

The Lingphi bounces from one camera to the next, always one step ahead. Suddenly it vanishes. I stop and look around. Where's it gone? Then I realize the room is silent and everyone is looking at me.

'Well,' drawls Strider finally. 'Are you trying to impress me with your free-running skills? Or are you just trying to break something?'

'I think he's gone mad,' someone mutters.

'I was, I—' I rack my brain, searching for an excuse. 'I—'

Strider's eyes narrow. 'If I were you, Finn, I would go back upstairs and not say another word. Get on your marker and thank your lucky stars nothing broke.'

'Right. Got it,' I say.

'Not another word,' he says, more sharply this time.

With every eye burning into me, I walk upstairs. I stand on my marker at the back of the shop.

'What the hell was that about?' whispers Richie.

At last an answer comes to me a minute too late. 'A rat,' I say.

Richie's eyes widen and he looks around the room. 'I hate rats.'

It takes another twenty minutes to get everything ready for the shot. All the while, I look out for the

Lingphi. I don't see anything. Perhaps he's given up for today, and as much as I doubt it deep down, I cling to that thought.

'This is an expensive shot, so we're only doing two takes,' says Richie.

'So . . . no pressure then.'

'None at all. Just if you blow it, the whole film will collapse.'

I laugh and he grins. 'And try not to drop this,' he adds, handing me the forbidden jewel.

Moving backwards out of shot, he waits for me to give him the thumbs up, before lifting his arm in the air.

'Scene 31. Cameras ready? Lights ready? Sound ready? Take one,' booms a voice.

Forget about the demon! Think only of the stunt!

'Three, two, one, action.' Richie's hand drops.

I take a deep breath, grip the jewel even tighter, and run for the glass panel stretched across the shop front. Halfway there, my foot lands on the plate of the air ram, it launches me upward and I'm catapulted through the air my body hurtling towards the glass. It's like I'm flying. Milliseconds before I touch the window, someone sets off mini explosions. The window shatters. My body soars through the air to the crash mat below. Slamming my eyes shut, I roll over the mat, fragments of glass pouring over me, the jewel still in my hand.

'And cut!'

Everyone starts cheering. I did it! And it went so well.

With my eyes still closed, I climb to my feet and feel fingers pull off pieces of the window. As it was safety glass, it was four times as thick as normal and broke into relatively harmless fragments. Apparently they're more round than sharp.

'That was fantastic,' says Strider.

'You can open your eyes now,' says Jenks. 'We've got the glass off your face.'

It takes a further five minutes for Richie and Jenks to make sure every piece of glass is off my hair, skin, and clothes. It's weird. We've been waiting for over three hours to do this stunt and the whole thing took less than thirty seconds.

'Come here, see yourself on screen,' says Strider.

Standing behind him, I watch the playback on a computer. Whoa! It really looks as if I smashed into the glass, even though I didn't touch it.

'Ready to do it again?' he asks.

'Absolutely.'

An hour later, the cameras and explosions are reset and all the fragments have been picked off the floor. Another glass panel has been put into place and I'm ready. I take a look at the set again; just to make sure the Lingphi hasn't arrived. Then I notice Calum glaring at me from the shadows. What's he doing here? This isn't his shoot.

'Three, two, one, action.'

I have to forget about Calum. I run for the glass, my foot springing off the air ram. Catapulted upwards, a black shadow and two amber eyes appear. They glint cruelly.

I'm hurtling towards the window. There's no way I can stop.

CHAPTER 18

My body hits the glass, pain shudders through me, air sucks from my lungs, and I drop the jewel. The glass smashes and I crash onto the mat. Thin shards rain over me, slicing into my skin, as I roll over and over before at last coming to a stop.

'Cut!' bellows the director.

Perfect choice of word!

I black out.

*

'He's not as bad as we first thought.'

The words sound fuzzy.

'He was so lucky.' There's a deep sigh. 'When I think about what could have happened.' Is that Jenks?

'I just don't get how this could have gone on,' says someone who sounds like Strider. 'How could the glass have been swapped?'

They sound distant. I try to concentrate.

'The police have spoken to everyone on set and no one knows a thing. No one saw a thing.' Is Marcus here too? 'They think it wasn't foul play though. They think the company sent the wrong glass in the first place.'

'You would have thought a technician would notice the difference in weight,' says Strider.

'I oversaw the whole stunt and I didn't notice anything different,' says Jenks.

I shuffle slightly and open my eyes.

'He's awake,' says Marcus. His head appears straight in my line of vision. 'How are you feeling?'

'Where am I?' I croak, my throat dry.

'In hospital.'

I bolt upright. Then freeze. My muscles ache. Heart monitors, drips, and other strange equipment fill the room, but thankfully none are attached to me.

'Hey, take it easy,' says Strider. 'Nothing's broken, but you took one hell of a bang.'

'What happened?'

'You smashed straight through the window. For some reason, the explosions didn't detonate and it was the wrong glass.'

'You were so lucky. The padding saved you,' says Jenks. 'None of the glass went too deep and you didn't need stitches.'

I snort quietly. I don't feel lucky. 'How did I get here?'

'By ambulance. There was so much blood, we thought it was a lot worse.' Jenks shakes his head. 'Things have never gone so wrong on my watch before.'

'We're just glad you're OK,' says Marcus.

'How long have I been out for?'

'A day. They gave you drugs to make you sleep.'

A whole day? 'What about filming?'

'It's been postponed,' says Strider. 'And that really is the least of your worries.'

'Oh God—you told my mum, didn't you? Did you call her in England? Is she on her way here?'

Marcus chuckles. 'No, we haven't called her. We talked about it and decided we'd give you a day or two to see how you are.' He hesitates. 'Do you want us to ring her?'

'No,' I say quickly. 'She'll only worry.' My head sinks back into the pillow.

'If you're feeling up to it,' says the director, 'there are two Thai policemen who want to speak to you. They're waiting outside.'

'It's fine. Let them in,' I say.

Within minutes, I'm alone in the room with two Thai officers. Their uniforms make them look like they're in the military rather than the police, and I can't take my eyes off the guns in their holsters.

'We are very glad to see you awake. How are you feeling?' asks the man holding the notebook.

'I'm OK.'

'That is good to hear. Now, just before the stunt, did you see anything suspicious?' he asks.

'What like?' I ask. Amber eyes . . .

'Anything. It has been reported that you were behaving strangely. You were chasing something. According to'— he checks his notebook—'Richard Brown, you said there was a rat.'

I lick my dry lips. This is the moment I could be truthful. But what if they think I'm mad? Will I be taken to a different type of hospital? They are from Thailand though, so perhaps they know about the Lingphi.

'Do you believe in curses or creatures that can be summoned?' I say.

The policemen look at each other before back at me.

The second policeman sighs. 'I know there are many rumours flying about this film, but there are no such things as curses. What were you chasing?'

'A rat.'

✳

Three hours later, I'm in a limousine pulling up to the bungalow. We dropped Strider back at the studio, as he wanted to look around the warehouse again.

I grab the handle to open the car door, when Marcus says, 'Finn.'

I pause.

'I was wondering whether you'd like to live with me and Blake during filming, rather than here?'

'What?'

Even Jenks looks curious.

'Let me explain,' says Marcus. 'I feel responsible. You're here because you're a stunt double to my son and you've ended up in hospital.'

For a moment I play with the idea. I'd be away from Calum . . . but then I would be with Natasha. 'It's not your fault. I seem to attract disasters,' I say finally. 'I think I should stay with my stunt team.'

'All right,' he says, looking slightly disappointed. 'But if you change your mind, you know where we are.'

As soon as the limo rolls away, Jenks rounds on me. 'Why on earth would you rather stay with us than live in luxury with the Saunders?'

'Have you met Natasha?'

'Yes, loads of times and she's lovely.' He doesn't even sound sarcastic.

'Are you having a laugh?'

'No. She's one of the most maternal women I've ever met.'

'Not to me, she isn't.'

Jenks opens the door and gestures for me to go in first. The rest of my stunt team are huddled in a semicircle around a laptop on the breakfast counter.

'Finn, you're back,' squeals Lucy, jumping up from the barstool.

'How are you feeling?' says Richie, pushing Calum out of the way, walking straight over to me.

'All right.'

'I wanted to come to the hospital but they said I was better off waiting for you here.' Richie tilts his head. 'You do look remarkably well considering you jumped through glass.'

Tom taps the laptop. 'We've been watching your stunt. The AD sent it over and it looks so real.'

'That's because it is real,' I mutter.

'You want to take a look?'

'I doubt he wants to,' says Jenks.

'Actually, I do.'

They part for me and rewind my scene. I watch myself hurtle through the air and my body collides with glass. Fragments shatter everywhere and I can't believe the amount of blood.

'I think the AD and Strider are hoping you'll let them use this footage in the film,' says Richie.

'That's not exactly ethical,' says Jenks.

'At least it wouldn't be a waste,' I say, when something occurs to me. It's a slim chance, but still a chance. 'Can you rewind it? I want to see it again.'

'You're in danger of becoming as vain as Blake,' says Richie.

'Or Calum,' adds Lucy.

'Hey!' Calum hits her on the back of the head. 'I'm not vain. I'm just honest about my abilities.'

The others groan, while I concentrate on the screen. This time I don't look at myself. I search the shadows for a sign of a hairy creature. Nothing. I'm not really surprised. It's supposed to be invisible.

'And Jenks, I want to offer my services,' continues Calum. 'If Finn needs to stay home tomorrow, I can be Blake's stunt double.'

What? I tear my eyes away from the screen.

Jenks shakes his head. 'If Finn needs a day off, Lucy will do his stunts. You're too big.'

'Who says I want a day off? I'm fine.'

'If I were you, I'd want a day off,' says Tom. 'In fact I might leave the movie altogether. More and more locals are saying it's cursed. They're pulling out of being Extras. Some of the film crew are getting skittish too and not just those from Thailand.'

'It sounds like you're one of them,' says Jenks.

Calum puts his arm around my shoulder. 'I've just had a thought. What if the film isn't cursed at all? What if it's Finn that's cursed?'

I twist out of his grip, his words shooting through me. Could Calum be right? Has the Lingphi been after me all this time? And that's why I can see it? That sort of makes sense, but who would summon a demon to hurt me?

'I hope nothing bad happens to you tomorrow,' adds Calum, his eyes glinting.

My body tenses. 'What were you doing on set anyway? You weren't supposed to be there.'

'I finished my scenes early and wanted to watch.'

Watch what, exactly?

I head to my room and sit in the only place available—my bed—when my phone pings. It's from Sam.

Apparently a flesh-eating zombie film is not a good film for a first date.

Mel has no taste.

Unlike the zombies, who taste flesh!!! I burst out laughing and relish the release of tension. I think Sam might be the only person in this world keeping me sane right now! Why couldn't Calum be a bit more like him? I have to spend so much time with him on the stunts, that it would be great if—

Oh God! A coldness grips my core.

Calum's been there every time something's gone wrong.

CHAPTER 19

Two hours later, Richie, Jenks, and I head to the Thai Orchid for dinner.

'Where are the others?' I ask. *And when I say others I mean Calum.*

'Lucy and Tom went to ballet class,' says Jenks.

'What class?' I stop walking. 'Tom does ballet?'

'I've done ballet in the past,' says Jenks.

I stare at the squat muscular man in front of me. 'You?'

'Yeah, it's fantastic for fitness and discipline. You should try it.'

Wow—Mum was right. 'What about you, Richie?'

He snorts. 'I'm no good at it.'

'Is Calum at ballet too?'

Jenks shakes his head. 'No, he should be at the restaurant already. He got there early as he was so hungry.'

As soon as we walk in, I spot Calum sitting alone at a table for two. This is the perfect chance for me to talk to him on his own but I need to get to that seat before someone else does. Then I see the long queues for food. Damn.

'Excuse me, would you mind if I squeeze through and get some prawn crackers?' I ask a cameraman, who's at the front of one of the buffet stations.

'Sure. Why not?'

I heap crackers onto my plate and hurry across the room.

'Nice to see you're looking after yourself,' says Richie, raising an eyebrow.

'I'm not that hungry. I ate in the hospital.'

I wait until Richie joins the back of a line before dropping into the seat opposite Calum.

'What are you doing here?' he asks, his lip curling.

'I want to know how you control the Lingphi,' I say quietly.

'The what?'

'The Lingphi.'

He looks at me blankly and I almost laugh. Is he honestly going to deny it? I've spent the last hour working out how it's got to be him. 'You've been there every time something's gone wrong in this film. You were there when the glass was swapped. You were there when the horse was spooked and when my vine broke. You even tried to say it was my weight that broke it, covering the Lingphi's tracks.'

'You think someone's sabotaging things?' Calum's eyes widen. 'I thought they were accidents, but—'

'The only thing I don't get is the wire. Why did it trip you up?' Then I gasp. It's like a light bulb pings in my head. 'It wasn't meant for you, it was meant for me, wasn't it? That's why you were so angry about it.'

His mouth drops open. 'The wire was meant for you instead of me? *You* should have missed that stunt?'

'So you admit it then?'

'Admit what?' He looks at me as if I'm going mad.

'Tell me one thing,' I say, leaning forward. 'Are you trying to get the Lingphi to hurt me? But why? Do you want me to leave Thailand?'

'Will you stop going on about a Lingf-thing?'

'Because if it's just me, why Will and Dan? And why have other things broken on set too?'

Calum waves his ice cream spoon in the air. 'I honestly have no idea what you're talking about. But if you're asking me if I'd like you to get off the film—then, yes, I would.'

He gives me such a poisonous glare, I'm silent for a second.

'Why do you hate me so much?' I ask at last.

He puts down his spoon. 'It's not you exactly. It's what you represent. I had to work so hard to get into the stunt academy. I had to train and train, then wait until I was the right age, like everyone else. But oh no—not you! You get to go at fourteen. And even though you just scrape through—you can't ride a horse, you were at the bottom of almost everything—you still pass. And then you get the role of every stuntman's dream. You get to play an action hero on a major film franchise. I was the best on that course—and you know it—but all I get is bit parts. They say in Hollywood it's not what you know, it's who you know. And that's you. You're friends with Blake Saunders so Marcus bends over backwards to get you on this film set. I bet you didn't even have to audition.'

His words shatter against me like the pane of glass. Am I as lucky as Blake? I always thought he got things handed to him on a plate because of his dad. But perhaps I have too, without even realizing.

Calum shakes his head. 'If you're expecting an apology cos I've given you a hard time, you're not getting one. I've had a far harder time getting to where I am today than you.'

I swallow, a curious mixture of sympathy and guilt beginning to merge in my stomach, when suddenly I hear a cackle. Both emotions vanish.

'You summoned the Lingphi here?'

'What is a Lingphi?'

I look over my shoulder at the hairy cackling monkey. It seems to pose in front of its own painting, like its taunting me. It scampers over the buffet counter.

My eyes dart back to Calum. I have to say I'm impressed.
He isn't paying the creature the slightest bit of attention.

'What's it going to do?' I ask.

'What's what going to do?'

The Lingphi swings from light to light across the
restaurant, until it lands on our table. Still Calum refuses
to look at it.

'You should be an actor, not a stuntman,' I mutter.

'I have thought about that.' Then he clears his throat
and his cheeks redden. 'Not that I'd tell you anyway.'

The Lingphi leans back its head and spits a huge
globule onto Calum's bowl of ice cream. I watch in horror
as Calum scoops up the saliva-covered dessert and eats it.

'You really don't know,' I whisper.

'Know what?'

I grab the Lingphi by the scruff of its neck before it
has a chance to move. 'Who are you working for?'

The Lingphi bites my arm and I flinch, my fingers
letting go. It wriggles backwards and bears its teeth into a
wicked grin. Then hurtles out of the door.

'I'm working for Strider and Jenks, just like you,' says
Calum, looking at me like I've grown three heads.

'What? Why are you even telling me that?'

'Because I'm answering your question, you freak.' He
shakes his head at me again, then scrapes back his chair
and walks out of the restaurant.

I remain in my seat, rubbing my arm. If Calum's not
controlling the Lingphi, then who the hell is? At last,

Richie appears at my table. I've no idea how long I've been sitting here.

'You ready to go? Eaten enough crackers?' he asks.

My eyes dart to the full bowl in front of me. 'I'm really not hungry,' I say.

On the way home, I walk ahead of Richie and Jenks. That way they can still see me, but I'm not with them. I need space to think and for the first time I can't wait to be in my tiny room. Under a street light up ahead, I spot a parked black limo. The windows are open and it's not hard to work out who it belongs to.

'What do you mean you asked him to live with you?' says Natasha from inside.

'That boy's been through a lot,' says Marcus.

'That's because he attracts trouble. We don't want him hanging around Blake.'

'No. You don't want him around Blake. I personally—'

'I know what you personally want!' she snaps.

'Can you blame me? Finn is my son. My own flesh and blood. I have to. I need to—' The door opens and Marcus storms out.

I dive over a hedge into a front garden, my heart pounding, my head spinning.

'Finn!'

Oh no. I can't face Marcus now.

'What are you doing? You vaulted a hedge.'

I look up to see my stunt team staring at me. Marcus is nowhere to be seen.

CHAPTER 20

arcus is my dad . . . Marcus is my dad . . .
I lie in bed, those words flying around my brain. It's past midnight and I think everyone else is asleep.

Marcus is my dad . . .

Could it be true? There's only one person who can really answer that. Grabbing my mobile, I scramble out of the window and flop to the ground below. I can't talk in the house, even if I whisper. Someone could overhear and I shudder to think what would happen.

The grass is wet under my feet and I try not to think about snakes as I head to the end of the garden. I just hope I have phone coverage out here. *Yes!!!!* I dial Mum's number. She's six hours ahead in the UK.

'Finn,' she says, her voice husky. 'Is everything OK?'

I open my mouth but no sound comes out.

'Finn, is that you?' Her voice is clearer now. 'Finn?' Panic edges in. 'Finn?'

'Is Marcus Saunders my dad?' I blurt out.

Silence.

Then a whisper. But I don't catch what she says.

'Is he?' I ask.

'Oh God.' Her words are breathless and she doesn't need to say anything else.

The mobile slips from my hand and I stare at the bright screen on the ground as she talks. My brain can't compute what she's saying. Then she breaks down into tears before calling, 'Finn, Finn are you there?'

I drop to my knees and snatch the phone off the grass. 'Yeah, I'm here.' The words catch in my throat.

'Oh, love, I'm so sorry,' she says between sobs. 'How did you find out?'

My eyes begin to burn and I swallow hard. 'I heard him talking to Natasha.'

She swears under her breath. 'Does he know you know?'

I shake my head, then realize she can't see me. 'No. And I want it to stay like that.'

'But . . . maybe you should talk. Now it's out in the open.'

'It's not exactly out, Mum. Only four of us know.' *Or does Blake know as well?*

'I should call Marcus.'

'No! No you shouldn't.' I grip the phone so tight I'm surprised it doesn't break. 'Mum, promise me you won't say anything. I don't want him knowing. I just want to get this film out of the way and then I'll . . . I'll deal with it.'

'But, love—'

'Mum, promise me. It's the least you can do. You've been lying to me for fourteen years. You can lie to him for a month.'

There's an explosive sob and I know I should feel guilty but her crying seems to make me feel worse. Angrier. Why should I comfort her? She should be comforting me. And before I know it, the words slip out. 'You told me I'd never met my dad, but I've met him loads of times. You said he left when he found out you were pregnant.'

'He did leave.'

'Did you know he was married when you started seeing him?'

There's a pause, then an almost inaudible, 'Yes.'

My stomach twists.

'But Finn, you have to understand I was eighteen. We were in a film together and he was this great big Hollywood heart-throb. He was twenty-one and swept me off my feet. I was in love.'

Suddenly I can imagine it—Marcus chasing her. Mum is so trusting now and I bet she was even more trusting when she was younger. My anger begins to change direction. She was only four years older than me when they dated and *he* was the one who was married. 'I hate him,' I say.

'He's still your father. He's—'

'Don't try to defend him,' I say, hardly believing my ears. Then it occurs to me—she's still in love with him. Otherwise why wouldn't she have gone to the papers and sold our story? We've been scrabbling around for money while he's been living the life of luxury with his other family. I think of how she blushes and swoons every time she sees him and my stomach twists even more.

'Finn, why don't I come to Thailand?' she says. 'We need to talk face to face.'

And suddenly all I want is a hug from Mum . . . but there's no way she can afford to fly out here. Plus, I'd have to deal with Marcus. And what about the Lingphi? What if it targets her? She has to stay away. 'Mum. Please. Let me finish the film and we can deal with it back in the UK.'

It takes another five minutes for me to convince her.

'I love you, Finn,' she says finally.

'I love you too,' I say, tears coating my cheeks.

I scramble back into my room and stare at the ceiling. How am I going to even look at Marcus? All I want to do is punch him. But unless I'm ready to confront him, I'm going to have to fake everything is fine. I'm going to have to pretend I never heard a word. Oh God. I'm going to have to pretend with Blake too. He's not just my friend, he's my brother.

✱

'You're very quiet,' says Richie, the following morning. It's another early start. I think I managed to grab two hours sleep, max.

We're in a tuk-tuk heading back to the rainforest, where we climbed the vines. Apparently Strider and the scriptwriters were inspired last night and they're adding in an extra scene. No one's quite sure what's involved. I feel like my head's going to explode. I know I should be looking out for the Lingphi, but at the moment I'm just trying to work out how I'm going to avoid Marcus and Blake who are on set today as well.

'Have you any idea what the stunt will be?' I ask.

'I think it involves weapons.'

I sit up. 'Really?'

Richie nods, grinning. 'That's more like it. Some enthusiasm and interest! I think there's going to be a showdown between Rio and the main baddie, which'll be good to watch. A showdown between father and son.' *What???* My heart starts pounding until he adds, 'Marcus and Blake battling it out.'

'Will Blake use the weapon or will I?'

'You, of course.'

125

My heart doesn't just pound, it races. I'll get to use a weapon against Marcus.

I'm hoping for swords.

CHAPTER 21

'Have you ever had a go at archery before?' asks Jenks, when we arrive ten minutes later.

Fake swords I've played with; lightsabres, I'm an expert; but the freaking bow and arrow? Richie watches me carefully and I remember his words: be honest, and so I shake my head.

Jenks looks surprised. 'Didn't your dad ever make you a set out of bamboo and string?'

'I don't know who my dad is,' I say automatically. Then my stomach tightens. *Yes, I do. And no, he didn't.*

'Oh! I'm sorry,' says Jenks.

I shrug casually, while my fists clench. 'Mum used to

have lightsabre battles with me, but we never got into the whole Sherwood Forest thing.'

'Very wise. Luke Skywalker would beat Robin Hood any day,' says Richie. 'She sounds like a cool mum.'

'She's the best,' I say, realizing that I still believe it.

Jenks smiles. 'Well, we've set up an archery range in a clearing near here and you can have a go. But if you can't do it, don't worry. You can't be good at everything, and we can work something out.'

I smile back gratefully.

'But what you need to do—which I know you can,' continues Jenks, 'is hold the bow while free running around the jungle. You need to flip and leap over trees while being chased by Thai warriors. Then Marcus appears, chasing you too. At the end of your sequence, you shoot him.'

'Do I kill him?'

Jenks chuckles. 'This isn't the end of the film. You only get his leg.'

Damn!

✳

It turns out that I'm even worse at archery than I am at horse riding. How can something that looks so simple be so tricky? Robin Hood has gone up in my estimation.

'You need to relax,' says Richie, which is hard when half the film crew, including Calum, are watching.

My fingers shake as I pull back the string. Looking

down the arrow, I stare at the circular target fifteen metres away. *What if it's Marcus's head?* I take a deep breath and release the arrow. It doesn't even make the full distance, dropping limply to the floor. My jaw clenches. Richie hands me another arrow and I line it up again with the target, pulling the string back.

'His pose is good,' calls a rich deep voice.

I turn around startled, the arrow pointing at Marcus's heart.

'Whoa! You look like you want to kill me,' he says jokily.

Blake's beside him and my body grows hot. I feel dizzy, weak. This is my dad and brother. I've seen them so many times before but now it's different.

'You should never aim at someone unless we're filming,' says Richie, pressing down on the arrow so it lowers.

'It's not as if it would reach,' says Calum, sniggering.

Marcus walks towards me, his feet crushing the grass and leaves. 'Do you want me to help? I taught Blake until he had professional lessons.'

My insides seem to erupt. *Of course Blake had professional lessons. He's had every lesson going.*

'We used to play Robin Hood in the garden. Do you remember, Blake?' says his dad. My dad.

It's like the arrow's twisting inside my gut and I feel a bubble of anger growing and spewing inside me. My hands start to shake and the arrow slips from my grip.

'I could do with a break,' I whisper.

Richie's watching me carefully again. 'Good idea. And actually we need to go through your free-running sequence. Jenks has been mapping it out for you.'

I lift up my foot, suddenly wanting to stamp on the arrow, but I force myself to step over it. Keeping my eyes on the ground, I walk out of the clearing.

'Is he OK?' I hear Marcus ask.

Oh? So now you're concerned? Don't even bother. You're far too late.

Jenks has given me a lot of freedom, just showing me where I need to go and where I need to end up. I can choose any way of getting from A to B to C. Flinging myself over branches and kicking off tree trunks is great for releasing the anger and soon I feel almost like me again.

'You are amazing for your age,' says one of the Thai warriors, who's been practising with me.

'He is amazing for any age,' says another. 'I could hardly keep up with him. You will need to slow down for Marcus.'

A grin breaks out across my face and it feels strange. This might be the first time I've smiled all day.

'That was brilliant,' says Richie. 'Fancy another go at archery?'

Right now I feel as though I could conquer the world. 'Definitely,' I say.

We head back to the clearing and I stop. *You have got to*

be kidding? The anger bubbles inside me again. What is *she* doing here? Blake aims the bow again and hits the bullseye. The film crew cheer, Strider and Calum the loudest.

'Seventh one in a row,' yells Marcus, pumping his arms into the air.

'And I got it on film,' squeals Natasha, beaming and waving a camera.

They look like the perfect happy family. A runner hurries towards Natasha, handing her a bottle of water.

'Thank you,' she says. 'You're a star.'

Instantly I think of Mum. No one hands her anything. She has to get it herself. And looking at Natasha in her perfect make-up and obvious designer clothes, I feel like I want to explode. Richie puts his hand on my shoulder and I jump, before twisting out of his grasp.

'You can't compare yourself to Blake with archery. Marcus said he had lessons,' he says softly.

'I don't care about the archery,' I hiss.

'Then what do you care about?' Richie pauses, his eyes darting between the perfect happy family and me. 'Finn, I'm not only your guardian and teammate, I'm also your friend, and you look like you could seriously do with someone to talk to.'

Could I tell someone? Because I'm sick of bottling it up. Richie said I could trust him.

I open my mouth, when my stomach drops. With all the madness going on inside my head, somehow I forgot about the Lingphi. The black hairy monkey scampers across the clearing. *What's it going to do? What can I do to stop it?* Then it lands on Natasha's shoulder for a split second before leaping off and she beams even more.

Oh God!

Is Natasha in control of it?

Because if she is, no wonder it's trying to hurt me.

She's got a great motive.

CHAPTER

22

'Hey, Finn, you having another go?' says Blake, looking over at me. 'Or are you afraid I'll show you up?'

I'm afraid your mother will have me killed.

'Actually, Finn, I'd like to watch you use the bow. I missed seeing you earlier,' says Strider. 'This way I can compare you both.'

There's really nothing to compare, I think, but Strider's the director and what he says goes. Walking towards him, I scan the area for the Lingphi, but it's disappeared again. Why would it appear and then vanish without doing anything? Under everyone's glare, I take the bow and arrow. Standing like Blake did, with my feet perpendicular to the target, I draw my hand back towards my shoulder, along my jaw line, and release. The arrow flies through the air. If this were a movie, it would hit the target, and everyone would leap up and down. But this is real life. The arrow flies to the right, missing the board completely.

'At least it made the distance this time,' says Richie.

'I guess,' I mutter.

'Hmm,' says Strider. 'That was a good effort, but the thing is we don't have any spare time to let you practise. So I've decided, Finn, you will do the free running and Blake will do the archery.'

'Yes!' says Marcus.

Was there really any doubt?

Natasha clears her throat, her eyes darting between all of us. 'Are you sure that's a good idea? I don't think Blake should be with a bow and arrow during the actual scene. I didn't mind him having a go now but—'

'He's been doing archery for years,' says Marcus.

'But people will be aiming at him. What if an arrow hits him?'

'They won't be real arrows. They'll have rubber tips,' says Strider.

Sniggers drift through the crew and Blake looks mortified. 'Mum, it's OK.'

If this was five minutes ago, I'd be laughing too, but now I know the reason she doesn't want him involved. I bet she's ordered the Lingphi to do something like swap a fake arrow for a real one. Is it supposed to go astray and hit me? Then my heart starts pounding. If Blake's doing the stunt, she'll need to find the Lingphi to give it new instructions . . . and if I follow her, I could find it. Then I give myself a shake. Is my imagination going completely wild? I know she doesn't like me, but that's a pretty big leap to murder.

My mind is still going crazy when Blake and I are herded into hair and make-up. The artists aren't here yet and so we're on our own.

'Sorry I took away your stunt again. I can't help being this good,' says Blake, waggling his eyebrows.

I snort. 'Are you OK in this trailer? Because there are some sharp scissors in here and I'd hate for you to get hurt. Do you need me to get Mummy to check on you?'

Blake's grin disappears and he drops his head into his hands. 'I can't believe she said that in front of everyone.'

'I paid her.'

Blake chuckles briefly. Too briefly. He looks up at me. 'In all honesty, Finn, she's driving me mad. She doesn't want me out of her sight. She's always been a bit paranoid, but now—'

'Things have been going wrong,' I say.

'Wow. Are you defending my mum? I thought you hated her.'

'Has she said anything about . . . what could be causing these things?'

'No. Just that we should go home.'

Maybe we should.

The door to the trailer opens and a make-up artist steps inside. 'You both ready to become Rio?' she asks.

*

About an hour later, I head for the vines, a quiver full of arrows strapped to my back. As it's only a one-minute walk, I'm allowed on my own. Blake left earlier. His mum wanted him for something, probably to cover him in bubble wrap. I step over a tree stump when I feel a hand on my shoulder.

'I'm so proud of you, Blake, doing the archery.'

'I'm not Blake,' I say, twisting out of his grip.

'Oh? Finn!' Marcus's eyes widen. 'Wow, you look so much like him.'

'I look like Blake looking like Rio,' I say flatly.

'Yes, yes of course.'

'I should get going.'

I feel the anger build up inside of me again. Wouldn't it be great to have a father proud of me? Not one that pretends I don't exist. I half want the Lingphi to show up because right now I reckon I could take it.

'You look ready for battle,' says Richie, when I arrive.

'If only we were using swords,' I say.

The cameras start rolling.

Throw your anger into the stunt, I tell myself.

'Three, two, one, action,' says Richie.

'He's over there,' yells a Thai warrior.

I turn my head. There are three of them, quivers strapped to their backs too. Carrying the bow in my hand, I run through the forest, leaping over roots, careering through ferns. A fourth warrior appears in front of me and I run up a tree, somersaulting over so I'm facing the other way. I hurtle through the undergrowth, vaulting a low tree branch. I swing under another before reaching a small clearing, and see Marcus's back in front of me. The plan is to run halfway towards him and then roll across the ground when he turns and spots me. At that moment, Blake and I'll swap. I step forwards when I hear a cackle.

What????

Not now!

I look up but can't see a thing. I take another step and there's a second cackle. I turn and see the Lingphi on a branch covered in leaves, a bow and arrow in its hands. For a split second I freeze. It's a weaponized monkey. And it's not aiming at me, but at Marcus. The Lingphi draws back its arm and suddenly I'm running across the clearing faster than I've ever run before.

CHAPTER 23

I leap forward, grabbing Marcus around the knees, and he slams to the ground with a yell. The arrow whizzes past and I scramble backwards off him. For a second there's silence.

Then Strider bawls, 'What the hell are you doing, Finn?'

'There was—'

'An arrow!' exclaims a cameraman. He darts past Marcus and pulls the arrow out of the ground. Then swears loudly. 'It's a real one. I thought we were only using these on the targets.'

The crew rush closer to see the steel-tipped weapon, when I feel two hands on my shoulder and I turn to find Marcus staring at me.

'You saved my life,' he says breathlessly.

'It was nothing,' I say, stepping out of his grip.

'It was not nothing. If that had hit me . . .' His words drop away.

'How did you see it?' asks the cameraman. 'How did you spot that arrow?'

Uh oh, I hadn't thought of this. 'I—I just saw it flying through the air.'

Suddenly I hear a gasp and a Thai warrior pulls a steel-tipped arrow from his quiver. 'Why do I have real ones in here instead of fake?' The other warriors check their quivers too.

'Someone must have swapped them. We should call the police,' says the cameraman.

'Now, let's just wait a second,' says Strider, putting his hand in the air. 'I imagine there was an accident with the props. Someone must have mixed them up by mistake.'

'That's a pretty big mistake to make,' says the cameraman.

'What do you think, Marcus? Do we need to call the police?' asks the director.

Marcus's eyes narrow, then he shakes his head. 'No one was hurt.'

Everyone in the crew looks nervous, apart from Strider who beams. 'Well then, I have an idea. Finn, your rugby tackle was brilliant and I think we should incorporate it into the scene. You should tackle Marcus to the ground and then have a fistfight. Jenks, could you choreograph one? We'll film it in a couple of days.'

Earlier, I would have been ecstatic to punch Marcus, but now I just want to keep him safe. I want to keep everyone safe. I don't even care about this film going ahead anymore. I just don't want anyone to die.

'Marcus!' Natasha's voice rings through the forest, as she hurtles towards us, Blake by her side.

Tears coat her face and for a moment I feel sorry for her. She can't have been behind it—she's far too shocked. Then I remember her profession—she's an actress—and I bet right now she's giving an Oscar-winning performance.

✱

That night I hardly sleep again. I keep expecting—no, hoping—to hear that the film is being cancelled. But in the morning Richie knocks on my door early for today's shoot.

'Come on, Rio,' he shouts through the door.

That's the nickname they're giving me, saying that I'm a real hero. If the Lingphi wasn't about, I might be able to enjoy it.

I open the door to find Richie in his pyjamas. 'How come you're not ready?' I ask.

'I swapped with Lucy. I'm not coming with you today.'

'Am I that bad to be around?'

'Trouble does seem to follow you around,' he says with a laugh. 'But no, that's not the reason. Lucy asked if she could swap, and as there's a strong possibility you won't be able to do the stunt, she needs to be there to take your place.'

'Why won't I be able to do the stunt?'

'You have read the script, haven't you?'

'Yes!' We're filming one of the penultimate scenes, with Rio escaping the warriors. 'And I'm fine with elephants.'

'You have to ride one and I remember your skills on the horse.'

'But we don't run. We walk and I'm all right on a horse if it plods.'

Richie grins. 'I'm sure you'll do fine. And to be honest, you could fall off, cause a massive stampede, and still be loved. You saved *the* Marcus Saunders yesterday.'

'Is he going to be there?'

'He's not in that scene, so no.'

Which means the Lingphi might not be there either. But what if it chases Marcus somewhere else? At least I can see the Lingphi and have a chance at stopping it. But it could be after me as well. Argh! My mind is going crazy. I wish I had someone to talk to. As much as I trust Richie, I'm sure he'll think I'm mad if I start talking about demons. He might even stop me from doing future stunts. Perhaps I could talk to Blake. *What am I thinking?* Blake, can I talk to you about an invisible creature that I think your mother has summoned to kill me or your dad. Oh, and the reason she wants to kill one of us is because Marcus is my father.

'Finn, are you still with me? You kind of spaced out,' says Richie.

'I'm good,' I lie.

CHAPTER

24

'Thanks for saving my dad,' says Blake, the following morning.

We're in a trailer on the edge of the elephant sanctuary, waiting to get back in Thai warrior gear. I'm trying hard to treat Blake normally. I need to forget that we're related.

'Anyone would have done it,' I say with a shrug.

'Mum thinks someone targeted him. She thinks the police should be involved.'

I look at him in surprise. 'Your mum said that?'

'Like I told you earlier, she's completely paranoid.' Then he stares at me and frowns. 'Are you all right? You look even worse than usual.'

'Thanks! I didn't sleep well.'

'Thank God for make-up artists. Although they might need a plastic surgeon to sort out your looks.'

An hour later, we're both dressed like Rio, standing in the dusty paddock of an elephant sanctuary with Jenks, Lucy, and Calum. I've scanned the area for the Lingphi, but it's not shown itself yet. I try to unclench my jaw. I'm fed up with not sleeping; I'm fed up with living in fear. If it comes, I'll deal with it, otherwise I'm going to try to enjoy myself today because I am in the most extraordinary place. I wish Mum could see it.

Just behind us lies a Buddhist temple, surrounded by golden statues of hybrid creatures and sea serpents. There are tourist shops and an outdoor cafe, catering for staff and visitors. A massive field is to the right of us, with trees dotted about, leading to a hilly forest with a river meandering through. It's where the film crew are setting up, frantically making sure everything's working and they've got the right equipment—not wanting another *incident*! But what really takes my breath away are the eight elephants in their stables. There are no doors, but each elephant is tied to a ring on the floor by a chain wrapped around an ankle. They're massive, wrinkly, grey, and dusty. Their eyes are haunting, so wise and knowing, as if they can see straight into my soul.

'I've always wanted to ride an elephant,' says Lucy. 'Are you sure you don't want me to do it?'

'I'm positive.'

'Ugh, they're just so big.' Blake shudders next to me.

'I thought you were good with animals. You were great on that horse.'

'Horses I know. But elephants are dangerous because they're unpredictable. One minute they're nice. The next they're wild.'

'Really?' I stare at the creatures a little more warily.

'Why do they have to be chained up?' says Lucy.

'Probably for that very reason,' says Blake.

My eyes drop down to the thick metal chains and I swallow.

'It is to stop them from eating everything in one day. They would eat everything in the sanctuary and we would have to shut down.'

I turn around to see a girl glaring at us. She puts her hands together and bows, but it looks like an effort, and it's definitely aimed in the direction of Jenks, Lucy, and Calum rather than at Blake and me.

'It's you,' I say, recognizing her scowl, as I bow at the same time.

'It's you,' she repeats.

'You two know each other?' asks Jenks, in surprise.

'She let me stroke one of the elephants' tongues.'

Jenks looks at me as if I'm mad, before shaking his head. 'I'm not even going to ask.'

The girl walks over to the nearest elephant and it starts snuffling her body with its trunk. 'The elephants can roam our fields at night, but if we let them do that in the day, the tourists would not see them and we would not get any income. And they are too domesticated to be released into the wild. They would not survive. That is why we need the chains.' She turns to look at us. 'So . . . which one of you is riding?'

'Me,' I say, putting my hand in the air. I drop it quickly. I'm not in school.

'Unless he falls off and I get a go,' says Lucy, grinning.

I wait for the girl to say, *He won't fall off. It's perfectly safe.* Instead, she says, 'OK. You both might get a go.'

Great!

'My name is Charn Chi, and what I say goes. You listen to me, not your director.'

As if on cue, Strider appears. 'We're ready when you are, Charn Chi.'

She nods and shouts something in Thai. Four men hurry across the paddock towards her, wearing old jeans, T-shirts, and sandals. Their skin is almost as leathery as the elephants', as if they've spent every day of their lives in the sun. They start unlocking the chains and, one by one, the elephants move closer to Charn Chi.

'These are the Mahouts,' she explains, pointing at the men. 'They look after the elephants. They will make sure you and the elephants come to no harm.'

'That's fabulous,' says Strider, turning to them. 'Thank you.'

'Where do you want the elephants to start?' she asks.

'In the field, by the large tree,' says Strider.

'The trees are all large,' she says scornfully.

Blake, Lucy, Calum, and I glance at each other. Normally people bend over backwards to be nice to Strider, hoping they'll get a part in a film. This girl looks like she couldn't care less.

'You're right. What a ridiculous direction,' says Strider. 'Could they start at the tree bent over like an old man?'

Charn Chi glances around before leading the elephants past us, and the mahouts follow behind, keeping the elephants on the right track. I have to stop myself from reaching out and stroking one of the beautiful creatures. I don't want to spook it. I sense Lucy tense up beside me and I have a feeling she's itching to do the same. Strider hurries after them onto the grass, but veers off to talk to a cameraman.

We walk towards the edge of the field. The ground is dry and cracked, the grass yellow and patchy, in desperate need of water. Then we stop and burst out laughing. One of the elephants has turned around and is scratching its backside against the trunk of the old man tree.

'Now that is happiness,' I say.

The elephant has closed its eyes and looks genuinely delighted.

'Blake,' calls Strider, gesturing him forward. 'We want you to pet the elephant, talk to it a bit. Then, Finn, you'll get up on it.'

A strong whining sound comes out of Lucy.

'Sorry,' I say.

'That's all right. I'm hoping I'll get a turn anyway.'

I throw her a dirty look. There's only one way she gets a ride and that's if things end badly for me.

'I'm sure you will,' adds Calum.

'Why are you even here?' I say. 'You're not filming.'

'I have a free day. And what better way to enjoy it than see you mess up.'

I turn my back to him and watch Blake as he walks over to the elephants, his normal swagger disappearing fast.

'He's terrified,' says Lucy.

'Do elephants smell fear?'

'All animals smell fear,' she replies.

Hmm. I didn't need to know that!

Charn Chi glares at Blake as he approaches and I'm pleased she doesn't save her hatred just for me. They start talking and Blake slowly lifts his arm, touching the elephant's neck. Another suddenly steps forward, swiping its trunk against Blake's back.

'What the—?' he yelps, spinning around.

'She just wants food, that is all,' says Charn Chi.

Lucy whines again. 'Charn Chi has my dream job.'

'Yeah. Because being a stuntwoman is really dull,' I say, laughing.

I can't help but smile. Twenty-nine takes. That's how many times they film the scene before Strider is happy with the shot. It's not the animals that are a nightmare. It's Blake. All he has to do is stroke the elephant at the front and talk to her, but he's jerky and nervous.

'Finn, you're up. And please say you're better than Blake,' says Strider.

My smile becomes a full-on beam.

'Don't look so pleased with yourself,' says Blake as we cross each other. 'It's harder than it looks.'

'It looked excruciating, so I hope not.'

'Shut up.'

As soon as I get close to the elephant, she opens her mouth. 'It's you,' I say, stretching out my arm, stroking her tongue. And I feel stupidly pleased that she didn't do this for Blake.

'Well done,' Finn,' calls Blake. 'You've impressed a girl at last.'

I smile until I see Charn Chi frown.

'I hope you are going to be better than him. I do not want to spend my whole day doing this,' she says.

'If I'm as bad as him, we might be here all night too.'

Her lips twitch, but then she straightens her mouth again.

'You're not happy we're here, are you?'

'You are paying great money to film the elephants. It will help feed them for months. So I am ecstatic,' she says flatly.

'Yeah. Your voice really shows it.'

Charn Chi glares even harder.

'How come you're in charge anyway? Shouldn't there be someone older?' I ask.

'My parents run the sanctuary and they are busy with—now, let me think—running the sanctuary. They asked me to do this.'

I look away from her and stroke the elephant. The grey beast is far nicer.

'Finn, we're going to practise a few times, get you used to the elephant before we start to film,' calls Strider.

Good! That means if it all goes wrong, no one can post it onto YouTube. 'How am I supposed to get up on the elephant?' I ask.

'Don't call her "the elephant",' says Charn Chi acidly. 'Her name is Shangri-La.' Then she lifts her hand into the air and says, 'Nap long.'

Shangri-La climbs down to her knees.

'Go to the right of her, stand on her leg, and use her neck and ear to pull yourself up.'

'Won't that hurt her?'

'You are tiny. She will not complain. She used to do this a lot before we rescued her.'

I'm not that tiny!

Standing to the right of Shangri-La, I whisper, 'Sorry,' before climbing onto her leg. I grab hold of her neck and ear and swing my leg over until I'm straddling her.

'Shuffle forward until you're behind her head and bend your knees.'

I scoot forwards onto her neck. This isn't quite as scary as I thought.

Then she stands up.

Whoa! My fingers grasp for the thick black hairs sticking out of her head. I'm really high up. I mean really high. My heart starts pounding. Shangri-La lurches forward and I grip even tighter. It's a strange swaying motion as she walks and not the most comfortable between my legs. At least I'm staying on though. Glancing over my shoulder, I see the other seven elephants lumbering behind.

'You are doing well,' says Charn Chi.

'Thanks,' I say in surprise.

'I was talking to the elephant.'

CHAPTER
25

We lumber round the field. Well, try to. Shangri-La wants to stop to eat every single tree, shrub, and blade of grass. Charn Chi keeps shouting, but it doesn't do much good.

'She is no longer used to giving rides, but I have an idea,' says Charn Chi, when we return to the old man tree. 'Nap long,' she adds, and Shangri-La drops to her knees.

My body slips forwards and I curse under my breath. I grip the black coarse hairs even harder.

'You could have warned me.'

'You should always be on high alert when riding an elephant. They are not predictable,' says Charn Chi. *That's just what Blake said!* 'Stay here.'

'Should I get off her?'

'Yes. Never be on an elephant without me.'

I swing my leg over the elephant, sliding down her body, and Charn Chi disappears.

'That was great,' shouts Strider. 'You're a natural.'

Even from over here, I can see Blake, Calum, and Lucy scowl. I stroke Shangri-La and, minutes later, Charn Chi returns with two baskets full of bananas.

'I will stay out of camera shot and hold the fruit. They are Shangri-La's favourite food. She will follow me to have one.'

As if to prove the point, Shangri-La pokes her trunk into the basket.

'Out!' snaps Charn Chi, pushing her trunk away. 'Good girl. Now you can have one.'

'Can I feed her?' I ask.

Charn Chi hands me a banana and I hold it out. Shangri-La curls her trunk around the fruit, her rubbery skin sliding across my palm. I'm surprised how cold it is. Her trunk swoops to her mouth and she drops the banana inside.

'This might be one of the best things I've ever done,' I whisper.

'There is something very special about elephants,' says Charn Chi, almost smiling. Then her face hardens, as if she remembers who she's with.

We wait until the cameras are set up, and Charn Chi has to keep moving the fruit out of reach of Shangri-La.

'What about the other elephants? Do they like bananas?' I say. It seems a bit mean we're not feeding them.

Charn Chi points to the largest animal, his trunk draped over huge ivory tusks. 'Kibble likes watermelon. They all have their favourite foods and when this is over we will feed and spoil them lots.' She pats Shangri-La's neck. 'Your director says it is fine for the other mahouts to be in the film. He just does not want Rio being led. He also wants you to climb on the elephant without me in the shot. If you tell her, "Nap long," she should listen.'

'Should?'

Charn Chi shrugs.

At last, Strider shouts, 'On your marker, Finn.'

I stand to the right of Shangri-La and Charn Chi walks ahead, taking care to hide the bananas. Suddenly I feel nervous without her next to me.

'Scene 108. Cameras ready? Lights ready? Sound ready? Take 1.'

'Three, two, one, action,' shouts Jenks.

'Nap long,' I say. Shangri-La waggles her ears, but does nothing else.

We really should have practised this.

'Nap long,' I repeat, louder and harsher than I would have liked.

The giant beast drops down to her knees.

'Good girl,' I say, climbing onto her right leg.

Grabbing onto her ear and neck, I swing my leg over. She lumbers to her feet and I hold onto the hair between her ears. Charn Chi dangles the basket and we begin to move. It was a good tactic.

I hear the other elephants trampling the ground behind me and I know they're following. I feel my body relax into the slow rhythmic walk. It's still painful between the legs but we're not lurching to a stop at every tree and tuft of grass. I don't think Shangri-La's eyes have left the bananas. Suddenly I hear a massive trumpet and the elephants' footsteps behind me turn to thunder. They charge past me. Shangri-La starts running too.

I swear loudly.

Grasping onto her hair, I hold on as tightly as I can. Heart thrashing, my backside crashes up and down. This is worse than on the horse. Who knew elephants could move this quickly? Then I hear a cackle. The Lingphi. I don't have to look around to know it's here.

Charn Chi yells, holding out the bananas, but we storm straight past her. The mahouts scream too, but the elephants pay no attention. I bounce about on Shangri-La's back, sliding left and right. If I fall, I'm a goner. Instinctively, I tuck my knees in and lean forward. We charge out of the field, following the stampeding elephants into the hills, into the forest. I duck just in time, missing an overhanging branch. Flattening myself to her head, I can hardly breathe. Higher and higher we go. Suddenly the other elephants scatter in all directions, leaving us alone. I spot the river. We're heading straight for it. I pull back on Shangri-La's hair, and just as her feet touch the bank she swerves right. She thunders alongside the river, bearing straight for a cave in the cliff. The river pours out from it, glowing almost aquamarine, like it's from another world. Even though it's beautiful, something tells me to keep away.

'Stop!' I shout, for possibly the hundredth time.

Why don't I know *stop* in Thai? Surely that should have been the first thing I learnt. She doesn't speak English.

'Nap long,' I shout suddenly.

Shangri-La freezes. My body's thrown forward. I cling to her hairs so hard I'm surprised they don't rip out. Somehow I manage to stay on, as she climbs to her knees. Now is my chance. I swing my leg over and slide to the ground. Scrambling away from the cave, I finally dare to breathe. Shangri-La clambers back up again and I think she's going to leave me, but she wipes her trunk delicately against my cheek.

'Is that a kiss? Are you saying sorry?'

I swear she nods although it's probably my imagination.

'It wasn't your fault. It was that stupid Lingphi.'

My muscles tense. I look around quickly, to see if the creature's still here, but like always the demon has disappeared. I stretch out my arm and Shangri-La lifts her trunk, opening her mouth. I stroke her tongue for a while, before I say, 'Come on. We better get you back.'

I don't expect her to follow me—after all, I don't have any bananas—but to my astonishment she plods on behind. I walk slowly and in pain. I'm sure I'll be walking like a cowboy for days. And then I stop. I don't even know if I'm going in the right direction, all the trees look the same. Then there's the throb of an engine.

The roar cuts out and a girl shouts, 'Finn, Finn!'

'Over here,' I yell. 'I'm over here.'

The engine starts again and a quad bike swerves between the trees.

'You're safe,' cries Charn Chi, coming to a stop beside us.

'You sound relieved. Or were you talking to the elephant?'

She mutters something in Thai. Then says in English, 'You need to get on quickly so I can take you back.'

'What about Shangri-La?'

'We own this land—she can stay out here. The elephants often come this way at night. It is their playground.' She pulls out an old fashioned walkie-talkie and speaks in Thai again. 'I am telling them that I found you. The film crew and mahouts are going crazy, searching for you. We will meet them at the entrance to the sanctuary.'

I try not to wince as I climb onto the back of the quad bike. Then I hesitate. Where should I put my hands?

'You have to hold my waist,' she says.

Feeling even more uncomfortable than when I was on the elephant, I grab her round the middle. We lurch over the bumps in the forest, but she artfully dodges the trees and soon we arrive at the entrance of the sanctuary where some of the film crew are waiting for me. I release her instantly.

'You will be all right?' she asks, looking around anxiously. 'I want to check all the elephants are OK.'

'I'll be fine. Thanks for coming to get me.'

She nods before disappearing on the quad bike.

'Thank God you're safe,' says Jenks. Then his eyes fly to the sky. 'I'm thinking that far too many times in this film.'

'Did you get the shot?' I ask.

'You are one crazy boy,' says Jenks. 'But yes, we did.'

'It's a powerful scene with you leading the stampede,' says Strider.

'I wasn't leading it.'

'Yeah, we know that, but the viewers won't!' He plants his hand on my shoulder. 'You should be pleased with what I'm about to say. We were supposed to come back for another day of filming tomorrow, but that won't be necessary now. We could never beat today's footage, which means you have a day off. In fact, the whole film crew will have a day off. God knows I need it. I was only watching and feel as though I've lost a life.'

'Do we know what set them off?' says Jenks.

'Apparently they do that sometimes. Just stampede out of nowhere,' says Strider. 'I wish they'd warned us.'

My jaws clench. It wasn't out of nowhere! Then I look around. 'Where's Blake? Where's Lucy and Calum?'

Jenks' mouth drops. 'I think they're still out looking for you. They don't know you've been found.'

Strider curses, then shouts to the film crew. 'Guys, we've got to go find Blake Saunders and the rest of the stunt team. They're still in the forest.'

'I'm coming too,' I say.

The Lingphi could be out there.

Jenks' eyes narrow and I'm convinced he's going to say no, but at last he says, 'You're coming with me then.'

As we head towards the field, I regret volunteering. My legs are killing me. Then I look to the right and freeze. The Lingphi is back, scampering across the grass. Charn Chi's arms pump the air as she runs after it, shouting in Thai.

She can see the demon too!

CHAPTER 26

A s soon as it's seven o'clock, I knock on Lucy's door. I'm still knocking two minutes later. 'Lucy,' I hiss, 'wake up.'

The door whips open and Lucy stands in her pyjamas, her face like thunder. 'There'd better be a good reason why you're waking me up on my day off. Is the house on fire?'

'I want to go and see the elephants,' I say.

'What? Are you three years old?'

'I know you love them as much as I do. I want to check they're all right after yesterday.'

'Charn Chi said they roam the forest at night.'

'I just want to make sure.'

Her face softens slightly.

'And if we go early, you might get a chance to feed them. You might even get to wash one.'

A smile cracks onto her face. 'What time do you want to go?'

'As soon as you're ready.'

I scribble a note for Richie and Jenks. Richie will be pleased he's not having to babysit me and I'm not breaking any rules. I'll be with a member of my stunt team.

✳

'Are you sure they're expecting us?' says Lucy, as I climb off the back of her moped, beside the tall perimeter wall.

I lied when I told her that I'd rung earlier. And now the wooden gates to the sanctuary are closed with a massive padlock dangling down.

'I think they've forgotten. I'll climb over the wall and remind them.'

'Isn't there a doorbell or something?' she asks, checking the gate.

I take three steps back before running towards the wall, gripping onto the jutting edges with my fingers, my toes scrabbling against the stone. I scuffle higher and higher, until at last my fingers hit the top. Dangling, I shout down to Lucy, 'Is there a doorbell or intercom?'

'No,' she yells, and so I heave myself onto the top.

The stables, the temple, and shops all look empty. Where would Charn Chi be? Leaping to the paddock

161

below, I land, knees bent, when I hear barking. Three mangy-looking dogs hurtle towards me.

'What's going on?' shouts Lucy from the other side.

I jump back onto the wall, grabbing at stone, my toes trying to find footholds. Glancing behind, I see the dogs getting closer. They're snarling, their heckles rising. Heart pounding, I scrabble upwards when someone shouts words in Thai. The dogs quieten and I turn my head again. Charn Chi looks even more furious than Lucy did first thing this morning.

'What are you doing here?' she demands.

My fingers release the stone and I drop to the ground, my eyes darting between her and the dogs. They bare their teeth and I swallow.

'Well?' she says.

'I saw you . . . with the Lingphi.'

Her eyes widen. 'What are you talking about?' she whispers.

'Yesterday. You were chasing the monkey—the one that started the stampede.'

This time it's her turn to gulp. 'You saw him? How? That is impossible.'

'Did you summon it?' I demand.

'Finn, what's going on?' calls Lucy.

'You are not alone?' yelps Charn Chi.

'It's the girl I was with yesterday. You need to let her in and set her up feeding the elephants, and then we can talk.'

Charn Chi nods, pulling a key out of her pocket. She says something to the dogs and they wag their tails. I hold out my fingers and they sniff me curiously. They're missing clumps of hair and look underfed. I'd have thought Charn Chi would have cared for them better.

'They are strays,' she says, as if reading my mind. 'We look after anything that wanders in.'

She unlocks the enormous gates and together we haul them open.

'Thank goodness, I thought you were being mauled to death,' says Lucy, looking at me. Then she turns to Charn Chi. 'It is OK us being here, isn't it? Finn said you were expecting us.'

Charn Chi flashes me a look, before saying, 'You are both very welcome. The mahouts are rounding up the elephants. When they have them back in the stables, you can feed them breakfast.'

'Really? That's brilliant,' says Lucy.

'First we prepare their food.'

Charn Chi shows us how to slice the bamboo with a massive knife and we grab buckets of watermelon, papaya, oranges, and bananas. Charn Chi keeps throwing me strange looks, but she doesn't mention the Lingphi in front of Lucy. By the time the food is ready, a few elephants are back in the stables.

'You can start feeding them,' instructs Charn Chi. 'Finn and I are going to look for Shangri-La.'

If Lucy suspects anything strange is going on, she keeps quiet. She dives into the bucket and hands some watermelon to the nearest elephant. Charn Chi and I hurry towards the field, bolting left.

As soon as we're no longer in sight of the stables, she says, 'How do I know you have really seen the Lingphi?'

'Well . . . it grows claws, its eyes shine amber, and it's tried to kill me many times.'

Charn Chi clasps her hands to her face, her eyes darting around. She looks nervous. No, not nervous. Terrified.

CHAPTER

27

Charn Chi's eyes drop to her feet. 'I never wanted the Lingphi to hurt anyone. Not badly.'

'Only hurt someone a little then?' I snarl.

She looks up at me, her face stricken. 'That is not what I meant. Not hurt them at all, just scare them so . . .' Her words fade.

'So . . . what?'

'How do I know I can trust you?'

'You're honestly asking me that? You're the one who set this *thing* on everyone or maybe not everyone, maybe just me.'

'It is not just you. Although he does seem to have taken a particular dislike but now I know why. It is because you can see him. You are a threat, a danger.'

I grit my teeth. 'Did you summon it . . . I mean him? Is that why you can see him?'

She nods slowly.

'Why?'

'My mother,' squeals Charn Chi.

'Your mother told you to?'

'No! My mother is here,' she says, grabbing my arm, bundling me behind a tree.

Peering out, I see a woman leading an elephant in the opposite direction.

'I am supposed to be working. We have to get out of here,' says Charn Chi.

Together we creep around the field, away from the stables, until at last we reach the back of a wooden house resting on stilts, with a steep gabled roof and balconies running around the perimeter. There's a driveway and another gate at the front leading to the main road.

'Shh,' hisses Charn Chi, even though I haven't said anything. 'Grandmother is asleep and we must not wake her.'

She leads me through their back garden towards some trees where there's a small yellow temple the size of two shoe boxes resting on a waist-high plinth. I've seen these around Thailand. Like the others, this one has a vase of flowers and a plate of fruit in front. Flies flicker about it, making my stomach churn.

'So why did you summon him?' I ask.

Charn Chi takes a deep breath and leans towards me, and suddenly I feel like I'm in a spy movie.

'Because of the film, *The Forbidden Jewel*,' she says. 'It cannot . . . it must not be filmed here.'

'You don't want your elephants in it?'

She snorts. 'I do not like the elephants being filmed, but I do not mind it.' She leans in so much closer, her breath tickles my neck. 'It is *what* they are filming tomorrow that I cannot stand.'

'I don't know what that is. I haven't seen the script yet.'

Charn Chi steps away from me and clenches her fists until her knuckles turn white. 'In the forest, close to where I found you and Shangri-La, they are planning to film in the cave.'

'Is that so bad?'

'It is the worst.' She closes her eyes and mutters, 'Please say I can trust you.'

'You can.'

She opens them again. 'This land has been in our family for generations and we are the sworn guardians of it. We have kept the cave a secret from the rest of the world because if people knew what was really here, it would be destroyed. There would be excavations. Pilgrimages. Thousands of people descending on the cave, trampling on it, searching.' Her lip curls in disgust. 'I cannot believe my parents turned their backs on their promise. They should never have rented out the land to *your* film company. Mother says we need the money to feed the elephants, which we do, but surely there is another way. Grandmother says it is not my parents' fault as they cannot see what is inside like she and I can. My parents think it is all make-believe.'

'What is inside?'

Charn Chi looks even more desperate. 'I should not tell you. Grandmother will kill me. But Finn, I do not know what to do. The Lingphi will not listen to me any more. I have no control.'

'You don't?' My gut twists.

'No! You think I want people to get hurt? I ordered the Lingphi to smash bulbs, ruin the cameras and cranes. I did not order him to use wires or swap glass. I did not want anyone to go to hospital. I just wanted people to think the location is cursed.'

'It's kind of working.'

'But not fast enough.'

'Hang on, if you're not in control, then who is?' I look around as if by some chance the Lingphi's master might pop out from behind a tree.

She lowers her head and whispers, 'The Lingphi.'

'What?'

'The ghost monkey himself.'

'The Lingphi is in control of his own actions?'

'Yes.' She looks at me, without blinking. 'I released him into this world and I cannot put him back. According to the legend, he will only leave if the reason for his summoning is fulfilled—if the location of the film is moved.' She clutches her stomach. 'People are getting hurt and I do not know what to do.'

Oh God! We stand in silence.

'So what are you trying to keep hidden in the cave?' I say at last.

Her eyes grow wet and she wipes them angrily. 'I am not that girl. That girl who cries.'

'What's wrong with crying? Better out than in, my mum always says.'

Charn Chi makes a short sharp half laugh, half cry. 'Have you ever heard of the Himmapan forest?'

I shake my head.

'Some people believe it is a place between heaven and earth, where mythical creatures live free from humans. Creatures like sea serpents, three-headed elephants, hybrids.'

'Like the sculptures around your temple?'

'And around Thailand.'

'OK . . . ?'

'The entrance to the legendary forest is in the Himalayan mountains. People have tried looking for it, but it is invisible to the mortal eye.' She pauses. 'There is another entrance too, a secret one, and it is right here.'

Suddenly my mind conjures up images of an aquamarine glow. 'The cave. I thought it looked weird with its glowing light.'

Charn Chi's jaw drops. 'You saw the glow?'

I nod.

'But you are not supposed to. Only seers can witness that; everyone else sees normal water.' Then her eyes widen and she gasps. 'Of course—you are a seer too. I thought Grandmother was the most powerful seer, but you must have even more "sight" than her. Usually only those who summon the Lingphi can see him. Grandmother has never seen him.'

'Does the Lingphi come from that forest?' I ask.

'No.'

'Does he come from'—I hesitate—'hell?'

There's a sharp intake of breath before she nods.

'So. You summoned a creature from hell?'

'I did not mean to. I thought he lived in the forest. Grandmother told me the story about the Lingphi long ago, how they do your bidding. And I have looked after ghosts so many times before I thought it would be easy. But this creature is not like any ghost I have ever met.'

'You've looked after ghosts?'

'A lot of people in Thailand do. We like to keep the wandering spirits happy.' She points to the little yellow temple. 'Normally they are for the spirits of loved ones, but this one is for the Lingphi to keep him happy.'

'You're trying to keep him happy even though he's hurting people?'

'If I don't, he might hurt us. I don't care about me, but what about my parents or my grandmother? She is sick and cannot escape.'

I stare at the flies burrowing into the plate of food on the plinth. 'What does your grandmother say? Does she have any idea how you can get rid of him?'

Charn Chi falls silent and kicks a loose stone. 'She does not know I summoned him. She does not know the creature is here.'

'You are kidding me?'

'She told me not to do it. She said it was too risky.'

'She was right.' The words slip out, but by the look on Charn Chi's face, I feel like I've slapped her.

'I had no choice. Can you imagine what would happen if the film crew found the entrance to the Himmapan forest? They would film the creatures and people from all over the world would come. Those sacred animals would no longer be free from humans.'

I groan inwardly. *She's right.* 'Are you sure the entrance is even here? Have you been through it?'

'We are the guardians, we are not allowed. But *you* saw the glow.' She clasps her hands to her face. 'I think fate brought you here on purpose. You can see the Lingphi, you can help me.'

'Fate didn't bring me here. A Lingphi trying to kill me brought me here.'

'Same thing,' she says.

Seriously? 'And how exactly do you expect me to help? You want me to catch him?'

'No, you would not be able to do so. But I have seen you with Blake. You are good friends. You can talk to him; get him to persuade his parents to move the movie. According to everyone on this film set, people do whatever the Saunders say.'

Perhaps it's her desperation or perhaps it's my own, because suddenly I find myself saying, 'All right, I'll help.'

CHAPTER 28

When we get back to the bungalow it's not hard sneaking out again. Lucy's in such a good mood, having fed and washed the elephants, that she's covering for me.

'Finn's got a girlfriend,' she sings. I let her believe it. It's easier that way.

I meet Charn Chi at the Saunders' house and she waits for me at the roadside while I go to the front door. I take a deep breath and ring the doorbell. At least I know Natasha's not trying to kill me now. A large shadow looms behind the glass.

'Finn,' says Marcus, looking genuinely pleased I'm here as he opens the door. 'How are you? Blake told me about your elephant ride.'

'I'm a little sore,' I say, with half a grin.

'I bet. And a huge thank-you once again for saving my life. I owe you.'

'Is Blake here?' I ask.

'Of course. Do come in.'

✳

Half an hour later, we're sitting in the Saunders' back garden on grass so perfectly cut it looks like AstroTurf. Blake stares at Charn Chi and me as if we are completely mad.

'You honestly think there's a ghost monkey trying to move the film?'

'Blake, think about it,' I say. 'The glass was swapped but no one saw how, cameras are faulty for no reason, someone shot an arrow at your dad. It all adds up.'

'It adds up to you being completely bonkers.' He shakes his head. 'You hear something go wrong and you automatically think, *I know—there must be a ghost monkey causing problems.*'

'I saw him. I saw the demon aim the arrow at your dad. How do you think I managed to spot it through the leaves?'

'Why did no one else see the creature?'

'Like I said, it's invisible to—'

'Everyone but you two. How convenient!' Blake stands up. 'Is this some sort of joke? Am I being filmed for a TV show—*How Gullible is Blake Saunders?*' He actually looks around as if there could be cameras lurking about. Then he stops for a second and stares at me. Cursing under his breath, he whispers, 'But the Ropen was real.'

'Exactly,' I say climbing to my feet. 'And the ghost monkey is real too. He grows claws, has amber eyes, and is covered in black fur.'

Blake continues to stare at me and I can almost see the cogs turning in his head. 'One crazy mythological creature being real I can believe. But two of them?'

'I know it sounds totally mad, but it's true.'

'And the only reason I can see him is that I summoned him,' says Charn Chi, standing up as well.

'What?' says Blake.

'The film *has* to be moved,' she says, and tells him everything.

When she finishes, disbelief oozes from Blake's face again and he snorts loudly. 'So, let me get this straight—we now not only have a demon ghost monkey, we also have a glowing cave that no one can see but you two?'

Somehow I stop myself from grabbing hold of him and shaking him. 'Listen, we're running out of time. The Lingphi is getting desperate and I'm really worried he's going to kill someone. It could be your dad, your mum, even you. He's gone for me a few times.'

'The Lingphi feels threatened by Finn because he can see him,' says Charn Chi. 'He could be the number-one target.'

'Why *can* you see him?' says Blake, looking at me.

'I don't know.'

Suddenly he sucks in a breath. 'Oh God. I know. Mawi said this might happen.'

'Who is Mawi?' says Charn Chi.

'The girl we met in Papua New Guinea.' Blake turns to me. 'She said that people who came in contact with the Ropen attracted mythical creatures. Beasts were drawn to them, fed off their energy.'

'The Lingphi isn't just drawn to me. He's drawn to everyone on this film set.'

'Well, maybe Mawi was wrong. Maybe it just means that you can *see* mythical creatures now.'

'You were in contact with the Ropen too.'

'But its blue gunk didn't seep into my back, my blood.'

I think of the pain and hallucinations after it happened. Perhaps they weren't hallucinations. More importantly: 'Does this mean you believe us now?'

Blake lets out a sigh. 'As ridiculous and far-fetched as this all sounds, it kind of makes sense. So. Do we need to tell my dad about it?'

'Sort of,' I say.

'What do you mean sort of?'

'Well. It's you, not we. And *you* can't tell him about the Lingphi or what's in the cave.'

'Then what can I tell him?'

'That the film location is cursed.'

'Dad's already heard that and doesn't believe it. Why can't I tell him about the rest?'

'Because as soon as a grown-up knows, the world will descend upon our cave,' says Charn Chi.

'Then what am I—?' His eyes suddenly widen. 'I could tell him that the land is sacred. I could tell him that it would be a PR nightmare if we filmed on it.'

'That is a brilliant idea,' says Charn Chi.

'It really is. When did you get so clever?'

'I've always been clever.' He pulls a face. 'But just so you both know—it's really doubtful Dad will change his mind.'

'If anyone can do it, you can,' I say.

✳

It seems like forever, but finally Blake returns through the back door. Taking one look at his face, I know it's not good news.

'He didn't believe you,' I say.

'No. He said that if the cave was sacred, they shouldn't have rented it out in the first place, and the producers have spent far too much money on this land already and won't waste it.' Blake drops onto the grass beside us, his face grim. 'I even told him that I thought the film was cursed. He laughed in my face, said I was superstitious. I told him one of us could get hurt and he suggested that I toughen up and become a bit more like you.'

I groan loudly and scrape my hands through my hair.

'So what now?' says Charn Chi.

I close my eyes, then open them again. 'I'll talk to Marcus.'

'What?' says Blake with a snort. 'You think he's going to listen to you rather than his own son?'

His words rip through me like the Lingphi's claws would, given half a chance.

'Anything's worth a try,' I say, feeling their eyes burn through me as I walk away.

I return to the front door and ring the doorbell. A familiar silhouette looms behind the glass and I swallow hard.

'Finn?' says Marcus, his eyebrow rising. 'I thought you were out with Blake.'

'I came to see you.'

'Me?'

'Yeah. Is there somewhere we can talk?'

'Ooh, this sounds intriguing,' he says, his signature smile returning to his face.

I follow him through the hallway into an enormous white lounge. A grandfather clock with ornate oriental patterns is the only splash of colour.

'Can I get you a drink or something to eat?'

I shake my head, already feeling nauseous. Perching on the edge of a white leather sofa, I say, 'Is there any chance you can talk to Strider about changing the location?'

Marcus's shoulders' slump and I see him bite back a groan as he drops into the armchair opposite me. 'Not you too. Are you going to tell me the land's very special to the elephant sanctuary?'

'It is special. It's sacred.'

'If it's so sacred, they should never have rented it to us in the first place.'

'They're wishing they hadn't.'

'I'm sorry Finn, but that's not my problem.'

'But just imagine what will happen if the press find out you knowingly disturbed a sacred cave. You took no notice of sacred land, stamped all over it, destroyed it with your machinery. It won't look good.'

'No one apart from the family thinks the land is sacred.'

'What if I let the media know—leak it to the papers?'

'You can't just make something sacred.' He shakes his head. 'If you came here just for this, I'm afraid you're wasting your time.'

'I saved your life. You said you owed me.'

'I was thinking more of getting you a moped, not moving a multimillion-dollar film,' he says with a laugh.

I can't believe I'm going to say these words. They taste sour and I haven't even uttered them yet.

I take a deep breath. 'I need you to move the location . . . Dad.'

CHAPTER

29

The room falls silent. Only the ticking time bomb of the grandfather clock fills the space. Marcus stares at me, blinking frantically.

'What . . . what did you say?' he whispers.

'I called you "Dad".' The words come out more harshly than I intended.

'What?' He clears his throat. 'What are you talking about?'

'You and my mum fifteen years ago.'

'Oh God.' His face drops into his hands. 'She promised me she wouldn't say.'

'She didn't. I overheard you and Natasha talking outside the Thai Orchid.'

Marcus scrunches his face. 'Have you rung your mother? Does she know?'

I pause. If I say yes, he'll contact her and they'll start making plans. He's spent my whole life lying to me, so I can lie to him. 'No, she doesn't, and I want it to stay like that until the film is finished.'

'Are you sure that's good idea?'

'I *know* it's a good idea.'

'Does—' he clears his throat again '—Blake know?'

'It's just me.'

He sighs heavily, falling back into the armchair. 'I loved her, you know.'

'Loved who?'

'Your mother. We met on a film set. She was so beautiful, had so much talent. I was going to split up with Natasha. But when I found out Natasha was pregnant, I couldn't leave her.'

'Mum was pregnant too.'

'I didn't know that until a few months later. And your mum was so much stronger than Natasha. I knew she could survive.'

'Mum was stronger than Natasha?' I shake my head in disbelief.

'Natasha's grown stronger, grown harder.'

His eyes well up and my stomach twinges a little. No, I won't feel sympathy for him. He doesn't deserve it.

'I'm sorry,' he says, wiping his eyes.

'For what? Being found out?'

'For everything.'

He looks so distraught, but then again he is an actor. Is this a performance or is he genuinely upset? My throat is drier than the Gobi desert. I wish I'd accepted a drink now.

Gripping the edge of the sofa, I say, 'I won't tell anyone, if you get the location of the film moved.'

'That's all you want?'

I nod.

'And if I don't?'

'I'll go to the newspapers, Twitter, Instagram, and any other social media I can think of. I'm sure there'll be lots of people interested in this story. You ignoring your son for fourteen years.'

'What's he doing here?' Natasha's words hurl towards me.

I turn to see her in the doorway, her mouth pursed and her narrow eyes glowering. 'What's wrong?' she demands, her attention turning to Marcus.

'He knows,' he whispers.

'Knows what? And where's Blake?'

'He's in the back garden,' I say.

'What's he doing out there? Is he wearing suntan lotion?'

'I told you, he knows!' says Marcus, thumping the arm of the chair. 'About me. About what I am to him.'

Natasha's face turns to horror as his words sink in. She swallows before spitting, 'Your mother.'

'Doesn't know I know,' I say, the slight feelings of compassion towards Marcus vanishing instantly. 'And before you ask, neither does Blake.'

She grabs onto the back of another chair and sways. Is she going to faint? Somehow she pulls herself round, so she's sitting in the second armchair opposite me, her eyes shining with tears. 'So what do you want?'

'He wants the location of the film moved,' says Marcus.

'That's ridiculous.'

'If you won't, I'm going straight to the papers.'

'You're blackmailing your own father?'

'Seriously? My own father who's really looked after me, who's been there for me all my life. I'd like to thank you for every birthday card I received. And it meant so much you coming to my parents' evenings. And those father–son chats have made my life so much easier.' I stare at the pair of them, breathing heavily. All those feelings I didn't even know I had, desperate to get out. 'Yeah, you've been hell of a father.'

Marcus leans forward, his hands together as if praying. 'I tried, Finn. I really did. I started the scholarship so you'd have a chance in life. Your mother told me you were passionate about acting.'

'The scholarship?'

'Yes. Without even seeing the audition tape, I knew you were going to win. I wanted you at the drama school. And when I saw the other kids treating you differently, I made sure Blake looked after you. I've done everything I can to land you jobs. You've had auditions because of me. Unfortunately you didn't land the roles—'

'Because you can't act,' says Natasha.

'Natasha!' he roars. 'How dare you?'

'Well, someone should tell him,' she shouts. 'It would be kinder.'

'Don't listen to her. You're a fantastic stunt double,' says Marcus. 'Finn, I've always been in the background. It was so hard seeing you grow up and not being part of your life.'

Their words scream around my brain, but I can't deal with them right now. Getting rid of the Lingphi and saving the Himmapan forest—that's all that matters. 'I've never asked you for anything,' I croak. 'And I'm not asking for money or a fancy house, or to go to a private school—anything else that Blake has. I just want the location of the film moved. If you get it done, we'll move on. We'll forget this conversation ever happened.'

He stares at me. And we both know neither of us can ever forget this conversation.

'We can't let this get out. I won't have this get out,' says Natasha.

Marcus exhales loudly. 'All right, I'll see what I can do. I'll call Strider and the producers. There was another piece of land they were looking at. I'll tell them that that's more suitable, and that it would be a PR nightmare if people found out we deliberately entered a sacred cave. I can't promise though. They might still say no.'

'You'll persuade them. You have to,' I say, climbing to my feet.

'Wow—you're more like Marcus than I thought,' says Natasha.

Marcus cracks a thin smile. 'One son has my acting skills, the other has my bravery.'

'You're not that brave,' I say. 'People think you're just like the heroes that you play in films, but I doubt any of them would leave a pregnant woman.'

He drops his head into his hands again, but this time tears spill through his fingers.

I hover in the doorway. 'I also want the elephant sanctuary to keep the money you've paid them. They need it.'

'What?' says Natasha.

'Think of it as all the money you saved on me—' I look at Natasha's designer clothes '—and that you saved on Mum. It's not as if you can't afford it.'

Marcus nods.

'I'll see you out,' says Natasha stiffly. 'Marcus, you need to make that phone call now.'

'If the film isn't moved by tonight, I'm calling the papers,' I say, walking out of the room.

Natasha leads me to the front door, but pauses with her fist clamped to the handle. 'There is one condition,' she says.

I almost snort. Is she honestly trying to bargain with me?

'Blake must never know about this,' she says.

'Don't you think he deserves to know the truth?'

'No! Blake used to go on and on about wanting a brother. He'll never forgive us for lying.' She looks so pitiful and so unlike Natasha.

'I don't know how I'd tell him anyway,' I say.

I close the door on her, my eyes burning. I just want to be alone, but Charn Chi and Blake are waiting for me. Walking almost in a trance, I step into the back garden. Blake and Charn Chi rush towards me.

'What have they done to you?' she asks. 'You look like they've killed your mother.'

'I told you he'd say no,' says Blake. 'I tried to warn you.'

I swallow hard. 'He didn't say no. He's calling the director and producers as we speak.'

'What?' explodes Blake, glowering at me, looking just like Natasha. 'My dad listens to you but not to me.'

CHAPTER

30

'Blake, don't start. I can't cope with this now,' I say.

'You can't cope?' Blake's lip curls. 'He's always had a soft spot for you, and now even more just because you do stunts. "Look what Finn's doing. Why can't you be a bit tougher like Finn?" Do you know after filming one scene, he said, "You are no Rio. You're style over substance. But Finn—"'

'Oh God, I'm sorry.'

'Can you imagine a dad saying that?'

'I can't even imagine having a dad,' I say softly.

'That's not my fault. And MY dad has always spoilt you!'

'Yeah, because you've been really neglected! You've had everything you've ever wanted!' I think of my cheap clothes and his designer ones. I think of my free school meals. It's never bothered me before, but now when I think about what could have been . . .

'Why should he spoil you?' says Blake, clenching his fists. 'As much as he wishes you were, you are not his son.'

Blood pumps around my body.

Charn Chi steps between us. 'Listen, guys, I—'

Sidestepping her, I say, 'You are a spoilt little brat who got all your big breaks because of Daddy. Everyone wants to please Marcus, get in with the Saunders—so you get the roles. You wouldn't be famous if it wasn't for him.' My throat thickens and I try not to think about the scholarship and my acceptance into stunt school. At least I know I got the role of Rio's stunt double by myself.

Blake sneers. 'You've always been so jealous of my fame and my fans. But you know what, Finn, you can't act.'

I want to hit him. 'You love being the centre of attention and can't stand it when anyone else is.'

'Go to hell,' says Blake, storming away. He stops for a second, looking over his shoulder. 'I hope something really bad happens to you on your next stunt.'

'Go back to Mummy and Daddy,' I shout, as he disappears through the back door.

'What happened in there with Marcus?' says Charn Chi.

'Nothing,' I say through gritted teeth.

'But they are going to move the film, aren't they?'

I spin around to face her. 'I don't know. I got Marcus to ring the producers and the director. What more do you want? Blood?'

Her eyes widen. 'I was only asking.'

'Well, don't.'

Barging past, I knock her shoulder, my whole body shaking. She yells at me in Thai and I think it's probably a good thing I don't understand.

Reaching the road, I have no idea where to go. I just want to be alone. And so I wander the streets for hours, my mind going wild. I take roads off the beaten track, seeing the real Hiva Hin, not just the tourist spots. I see houses propped up with corrugated iron. No glass in the windows, but old towels used as curtains. They stand crumbling next to grand traditional houses built on stilts. The rich and poor next to each other on the same road. Blake and me. Except we were never on the same road. But really, I don't care much about the money or the lifestyle. It's knowing a dad is there for you all the time. Knowing a dad would teach me to ride a bike, push me on the swings, come to sports day . . .

Somehow I arrive back at the bungalow. I push open the door and Lucy hurtles towards me.

'Thank goodness you're OK,' she says, before slapping me across the back of my head. 'You said you'd only be a couple of hours.'

My insides twist. 'I'm sorry, I forgot.'

'You forgot? You forgot that you have to stay with someone at all times? You forgot that I was covering for you? I'm now in trouble too, thank you every much.'

'Sorry,' I say again.

'Jenks, Richie, Tom, Calum are all out looking for you.'

My heart drops.

'I'll ring them. But if I were you, I'd hide in your room. Jenks is going to kill you.'

This is turning out to be hell of a day!

'Oh. And you missed all the excitement,' adds Lucy. 'We're not going to be here much longer. We're moving location soon.'

That should make me feel better, but right now I couldn't care less.

When Jenks returns, he stands in the doorway to my room, shouting and ranting. No energy to argue, I remain quiet. And with everything still buzzing around my head, his words are white noise. I just wish I could drown out Calum's sniggers coming from the lounge.

Finally Jenks throws a script at me. 'Tomorrow is a new day!' he snaps, before walking away.

A Post-it note is stuck to the top.

'If you think you can't do this, be honest! I won't mind. Calum and Lucy are more than happy to take your place.'

I bet they are. I read the script, and although it makes my blood run cold, there's no way I'm backing out of this one.

*

The next morning I'm shattered. Not only did I sleep badly, Jenks woke me up early so we could practise the stunt before most of the film crew arrived. Along with the rest of the stunt team, there are paramedics and a couple of firefighters. After all that's been happening, Strider isn't taking any chances.

Jenks is being nice, not acting like I disobeyed him. I think that's because the rehearsals are going so well. There's no sign of the Lingphi—he must have gone back to wherever he came from. Hell, most likely. So whatever happens with this stunt, at least I know I'm not going to be murdered by some demon monkey. The stunt is taking up all my brain space so I don't have to think about Marcus or Blake either. We practise and practise. The first time is terrifying, but with each go, it gets easier and easier.

At last Jenks says, 'We're filming the real thing in about half an hour. Blake's been through hair and make-up and they're about to shoot his scene. Stay here. You should watch to get your marker.'

I nod, but I want to bolt. I'm not sure I'm ready to face Blake yet.

I stand beside a cameraman, and as soon as Blake spots me, he sneers. It's the same look he used to save for me when we fell out all those years ago. A hand lands on my shoulder and I turn to see Marcus. Even though he's dressed as a villain and wearing make-up, the shadows under his eyes are unmistakable and he looks dreadful. I bet he didn't sleep well either. I step away. How dare he touch me?

'Have you heard we're moving?' he says quietly.

'Yeah.'

'It took some persuading. We've got to stay a few more days to finish the other scenes, like the Wall of Death—that's been fixed now—and our fistfight scene. But we're not going back to the sanctuary. We won't touch the cave.'

I glance back at Blake. If glares could kill, Marcus and I would be six feet under by now.

'The sanctuary will still get paid.' He hesitates. 'I'm paying them out of my own pocket.'

'Good,' I whisper.

'So our secret's safe?' he asks.

'Yeah. You need never worry about me again.'

Anguish flashes across his face. 'I've spent the last fourteen years worrying about you.'

'Well, don't.'

'In a way, I'm glad you know now. In the past it's

almost slipped out and I wonder whether part of me wanted it to. Maybe we can—'

I can't stay here any longer, whatever Jenks said. Seconds later, I'm walking down an empty street, cleared for the film, when a hand touches my shoulder again.

'Seriously?' I say twisting around.

But Marcus isn't standing behind me.

CHAPTER 31

'He has gone. You did it,' says Charn Chi, grinning madly. 'I put out the food last night and it is still there. He has not touched it. He must be back in—'

'Hell?'

She beams.

'This is great,' I say, trying to smile. 'Have you told your grandmother that the location's been moved?'

Charn Chi's face drops. 'I am not allowed to see her. She is even sicker. Mother is worried that I might pass on another bug to her.'

'Do you have a bug?' I say, stepping backwards.

'Lots of them—elephant diseases,' she says with a

grin. 'I hope you do not mind me coming to the set, but I wanted to thank you for everything. And to say sorry—I messed up so badly and did not know what to do until you . . .' Her words fade away.

'Not a problem. I won't say it's been a pleasure though.'

Charn Chi laughs and wraps her arms around me.

My body stiffens—a girl is hugging me—when suddenly I hear someone shout my name.

Turning slowly, I see Jenks standing at the end of the road.

'Get yourself over here before I pull off both your arms and beat you with the soggy ends!' he shouts.

*

Twenty minutes later, I'm sitting in the front of a tuk-tuk. It's different to the ones we've been chauffeured around in. A mini-truck instead of a moped pulls the taxi part, so there are foot pedals, a gearstick, and a steering wheel. I sit in the passenger seat while Richie drives. Cameras on moving vehicles are everywhere. Lucy is somewhere ahead, driving a tourist's car, while Calum operates the second identical tuk-tuk. The other cars in between us are driven by Thai stuntmen. I don't know their names yet. And way out of sight is the roadblock, barring the collapsed bridge, which Marcus blew up in a previous scene.

'Sneaking out to meet a girl,' says Richie, giving me a sideways glance. 'I wish I was fourteen again.'

'I wish I wasn't.'

He grins.

'Jenks treats me like a baby,' I say.

'He feels responsible for you and it's not as if you don't attract trouble.'

Not any more. The Lingphi's gone!

'You ready for this?' says Richie.

I nod.

'Then hold on tight.'

I clench the sides of my seat as we pull up to a junction. Richie slams his foot on the accelerator and we hurtle around the corner onto the motorway. He blares his horn and waves the other drivers to get out of the way. He swerves left and mounts the grassy bank to overtake a few. Swooping back into a lane, our tuk-tuk nudges Lucy's car. There's a squeal of tyres as Lucy wrenches out of the way, straight into another vehicle. Metal crunches behind us, and looking in the side mirror, I see the prang. Some cars stop, but Richie speeds up.

Only nine cars between Calum and us now. Sliding in and out of the lanes, we soon pull up beside the second tuk-tuk. My heart starts pounding. Even though there's no Lingphi, there are so many ways this stunt can go wrong. *Stop thinking like that!* The rehearsals were great.

Both tuk-tuks slow down. They'll edit to make it seem faster. Richie jerks inwards so there's only half a metre between us. I take a deep breath and leap across, my legs straddling the lanes, one foot in each tuk-tuk. I throw myself into the second vehicle and am about to fake punch Calum, when my blood turns to ice.

The Lingphi is sitting on the dashboard, grinning wildly.

How? Why? He shouldn't be here. More importantly, what's he going to do?

Calum looks at me, as if to say, 'Hit me.' He's supposed to slump unconscious and I'll lean over to take the steering wheel. But what if the Lingphi does something to him? What if his claws grow and he attacks? Without a second thought, I punch Calum as hard as I can, propelling him backwards. I shove him again, watching his eyes widen in realization, his arms flailing. He falls out of the moving vehicle, slamming to the ground. I look over my shoulder to see him roll across the tarmac before staggering to his feet. Thank God he's OK.

I scoot across to the driver's seat, when the Lingphi leaps onto my leg, slamming my foot down onto the accelerator. We speed up towards the roadblock. I grab him by the fur, waiting for his claws to grow. But to my astonishment, he lets himself be picked up. I throw him out of the vehicle. Why did that seem too easy?

Then I look forward again. I'm hurtling towards the roadblock and at this rate I'll crash through it . . . There's no bridge.

I slam my foot onto the clutch and brake pedals. Nothing happens. I should be slowing down. I pump the brake with my foot, but the tuk-tuk roars down the motorway. The Lingphi's destroyed the brakes. My hands grip the steering wheel, my heart thudding against my chest. The camera crew must be wondering what's going on. I'm supposed to have stopped. I should be on foot, running on the grassy verge by now. The roadblock looms.

Oh God. I need to do a U-turn, but at this speed the tuk-tuk won't make it. I hear a honk and look left. Richie's beside me, yelling wildly from his tuk-tuk. I can't hear a word. He gestures frantically, pointing to the side of the road.

'I can't pull over because I can't stop!' I scream, knowing he won't be able to hear.

CHAPTER

32

The blockade's even closer. I have no choice. Taking a deep breath, I leap from the tuk-tuk, my body crashing to the ground. Sky, tarmac, sky, tarmac is all I see as I roll across the road. There's a bang and the screech of crunching metal followed by an almighty splash. My tuk-tuk must be in the river. Richie slides to a stop next to me. Jumping out, he rushes to my side.

'Are you trying to kill yourself?' he shouts. I make to sit up when he yells, 'Stay where you are. Something could be broken.'

I freeze.

Then carefully wiggle my fingers and toes. Yes!!!

They're moving. And I can feel everything—pain throughout my body, blood dripping down my face.

'The brakes didn't work,' I say.

Cursing under his breath, Richie drops to his knees. Seconds later, sirens blare, and before I know it, faces fill my vision.

'Thank God you're alive,' says Marcus, leaning over me, stretching out his arm as if he's going to touch my forehead.

I instinctively recoil and he moves his arm back again, sadness flashing across his face. Jenks stands behind, peering over his shoulder, his face paler than I've ever seen.

Blake appears on my other side, falling to his knees by my head. *Don't give me a hard time because your ... our dad is here. I can't take it right now.*

'I didn't mean it,' whispers Blake. 'I didn't mean it when I said I wanted you to get hurt. I didn't want anything bad to happen to you. I'll make it up to you, I promise.'

Suddenly I feel something land on my leg. I lift my head to see the Lingphi snarling, saliva dripping from its fangs. My stomach drops. I kick frantically.

'What's he doing?' yelps Jenks. 'You need to stay still.'

'Get him off me,' I whisper, grabbing Blake's arm.

He looks down and his eyes widen. 'What the hell is that?'

'You can see it too?'

'Someone take that thing off Finn's leg,' shouts Blake.

'What thing?' says Marcus.

'That's the Lingphi,' I hiss.

Blake kicks at it with all his might. The creature's claws extend but Blake kicks again and the Lingphi scampers backwards. Feeling dizzy and sick, I let go of Blake's arm.

'Where's it gone?' says Blake. I grab his arm again and he gasps. 'I can only see it when you touch me.'

Turning my head, I watch the Lingphi's amber eyes flicker between Blake and me before he scurries away.

'Everyone out of the way!' yells a paramedic, looming over me. 'We need space. Only family members can stay.'

Everyone moves backwards and for a split second I wish I hadn't made it.

*

My injuries are superficial—that's what the paramedic said—which is good because I get to go back to the bungalow and not to the hospital. But I feel nauseous and in pain.

'You're probably suffering from shock,' says Richie as our taxi drives through the security gate. 'In fact, forget about you—*I'm* suffering from shock.'

'Have they looked at the tuk-tuk?' I ask.

'Yeah, the brakes had worn away,' says Jenks grimly.

I snort silently. I don't believe that for a second. The Lingphi messed with them and covered his tracks.

Jenks shakes his head and clenches his fists. 'I didn't think for one minute I'd have to check something like that. I assumed we wouldn't be supplied with faulty vehicles.'

'It's not your fault,' I say.

Jenks closes his eyes. 'I am the stunt coordinator. All the stunts are my responsibility.'

'Are we going to have to redo the shoot?' I ask, dreading the reply. I'm not sure I ever want to drive again after that.

'Strider wants to use the footage. Thinks it looks realistic, and, yes, before you say it—that's because it is real.' Jenks stares at me. 'You are one unlucky boy.'

Luck has nothing to do with it!

'If I knew you attracted this much trouble, I'm not sure I would have agreed to work on this film,' he adds.

'Thanks!'

'Finn, just promise me one thing: the next stunt you're in, don't get into trouble. Don't get hurt.'

'I promise,' I say, really wishing I could mean it.

Just as we pull up next to the driveway, Richie's phone pings. He reads his text, his mouth thinning and his eyes hardening.

'What is it?' I ask.

He clears his throat. 'Some people are saying it's sabotage. They want the police involved.' His face grows even grimmer as he adds, 'And I'm beginning to think they might be right.'

Jenks shakes his head. 'The police questioned lots of different mechanics extensively and they swear the brakes were worn away, not tampered with.' He grabs hold of the door handle. 'And thank God they were. Because if the brakes had been cut, this wouldn't be sabotage, it would be attempted murder.'

It is sabotage and it is attempted murder, I think, as we head to the front door.

For the rest of the day, I desperately want to see Charn Chi but Jenks won't let me out of his sight. I can't go to my room. I think he has an idea I'll sneak out and he even waits outside the bathroom door. I thought we were supposed to trust each other as a stunt team . . . although he may have a point!

I try getting Lucy and Richie to take me to the elephant sanctuary but I'm under strict lockdown and neither dares disobey Jenks. If only I had Charn Chi's mobile number. I have to tell her the Lingphi is still out there. And more crucially, I have a plan. Next time I see the demon, I'm going to grab onto an adult's arm and make sure they see him too.

Just don't let anyone else get hurt in the meantime.

CHAPTER

33

At seven o clock that evening there's a knock at the front door. I hurtle over, hoping it's Charn Chi.

'Marcus?' I say, in surprise.

He looks so wretched. 'Finn, can we talk?'

'Now?' I have far more important things on my mind.

'I thought I could take you to the Thai Orchid.'

If I go with him, I could sneak off to Charn Chi's. 'I'd better ask Jenks.'

'Of course.'

Ten minutes later, we're sitting at a table for two, bowls of chicken and noodles in front of us. Neither of us has spoken and I can almost taste the awkward. Marcus swallows. Perhaps he can taste it too.

'So . . . you wanted to talk?' I say. We need to get this over and done with if I want to slip out.

'Finn,' he says, his voice raw. 'I am so sorry I didn't tell you earlier. That was an awful way for you to find out.'

'Yeah, it really was.'

He shifts uncomfortably. 'I know you think I haven't been there for you—'

'Are you telling me you have?'

'I've tried as much as I can.'

I snort and he winces.

'I've watched you grow up from afar and hated myself for it. I wanted to be there for you. I wanted to—' He looks down and back up again. 'I made sure you had somewhere nice to live. I bought your mother a house and—'

'I thought Granddad gave it to her.'

'I did.'

'And you want a thank-you for putting a roof over your own son's head?' I can feel the bitter taste of anger rising in my throat.

'God, no. I just want you to understand that I have been present. Your mother sent me your school reports and we spoke every so often about how you were doing, what you liked and what you didn't. For example, I know you hate baked beans. I hate baked beans too.'

We both hate baked beans . . .

My eyes begin to sting and I put down my chopsticks. 'I used to dream that my dad would turn up. He'd come to the park and tell me how he'd been captured by pirates or been in prison, something or someone stopping him from coming to me. How it wasn't his choice.'

'It wasn't my choice,' he says quietly, his voice breaking.

'Was it Natasha's?'

He doesn't answer.

I bet that was the condition of them staying together.

We sit in silence and suddenly I realize the restaurant's filling up. My stunt team is at another table and Calum's glaring at me through his bruise-covered face. Yeah—I'm not surprised he's glaring. Richie sits next to him, his eyes darting between Marcus and me.

'You all right?' he mouths.

No! 'Yes,' I mouth back and he nods.

'Finn, I don't expect you to forgive me,' says Marcus, 'but maybe we could get to know each other a little better?'

Is that what I want? I look around the room, as if I'll find an answer, when my stomach spirals to the ground. The Lingphi is on the fish counter, grinning at me. I grab Marcus's arm and he puts his hand on mine.

'There,' I say, pointing to the counter.

He turns around but the Lingphi hurtles through the room.

'No, look towards the door,' I say louder. Marcus follows my finger but the Lingphi turns the handle and scurries outside. 'Did you see it?'

'See what?'

That wouldn't be his reaction if he did. My shoulders slump and I look down to see I'm still holding his arm. I yank my hand back, but Marcus is staring at me hopefully.

'I could teach you to fly if you like? Or to horse ride? Choose anything. It would be nice to spend some time together.'

'I'll think about it.' Flying does sound tempting. Then I glance through the window. 'Blake's outside.' I hesitate for a second. 'Have you told him about me?'

Marcus shakes his head almost imperceptibly. 'I think we should keep it a secret for just a little while longer.'

I'm still your shameful secret then!

I turn away in disgust and Marcus adds quickly, 'The more people who know, the more likely it will leak. And if that happens, the media will come at you and your world will explode.'

Is it your world or my world you're worried about? 'I only meant Blake,' I say.

He shakes his head again. 'Not just yet.'

'OK. Thanks for dinner.' I scrape back my chair and stand up.

'You haven't eaten.'

'Funnily enough, I'm not that hungry. Blake can take my seat and I'll go back to the bungalow.'

Marcus frowns. 'I shouldn't really let you out of my sight.'

'Why? You've been doing it my whole life.'

He winces again. Blake and I pass each other in the restaurant, but I don't have time to talk. Hurrying outside, I turn a corner and walk even faster. Then my insides groan. Why didn't I think this through? It's a long way on foot to the elephant sanctuary . . . and then I spot the mopeds parked against the wall. Isn't the blue one Blake's?

'Don't even think about stealing it.'

I whisk around to find Blake behind me.

'Aren't you eating with your dad?' I ask.

'No, it's you I came to see.'

'Listen I'm sorry I had dinner with him, but I haven't got time to talk about it n—'

'That's not why I wanted to see you. That thing on your leg, that was the Lingphi, wasn't it? It didn't go back to hell.'

'Yes, he is and no, he didn't.' I shake my head angrily. 'He was in the restaurant just now, taunting me.'

'Really?' Blake glances at the wall.

'I tried to get your dad to see the Lingphi. I touched his arm, hoping he'd see him like you could, but the demon bolted as soon as he saw what I was doing. I think he knows I can pass on the "sight".'

Blake lets out a long breath. 'Thank God we're leaving this place then. I'm thinking of asking Mum if we can go tomorrow.'

'Blake, we can't just leave that creature. We have to do something.'

'Why?'

'Because I can see him when no one else can. He could kill someone.'

Blake's face twists. 'I suppose you have a plan?'

'Not exactly. I'm going to see Charn Chi and hope she has some idea about what to do. So I need your moped. I'll bring it back to you tonight.'

'No way. You might smash it.'

'Seriously, Blake? That creature's on the loose and you're worried—'

'I'll give you a lift,' he says.

'Really? You'll help?'

'I'm just giving you a lift. Nothing else.'

'That's great. We need to go now.'

Blake nods, darting over to his moped and bending down to undo the lock, when I hear: 'Finn!'

Not again!

Turning, I see Calum stalking towards me like a lion about to kill some prey.

'Think you're clever, do you? Pushing me out of that tuk-tuk?' he snarls.

I step backwards. I might know martial arts, but I saw Calum at stunt school. He's much better than me.

'About that,' I say. 'I'm really sor—'

Suddenly Blake stands up. 'My dad loved how you threw yourself out of the tuk-tuk.'

Calum visibly jumps. 'I didn't see you there.'

'He was telling me and mum how your roll across the road was inspired. He said you have a great future in stunts. But'—Blake tilts his head—'are you saying it wasn't intentional?'

'Of course—of course it was intentional,' says Calum, throwing me a silencing glare. 'I thought it would make the scene look even better.'

'It did.' Blake pauses. 'Listen, I don't mean to be rude but Finn and I were just about to go.'

'Oh!' Calum looks awkward. 'Finn can't. Jenks sent me to get him.' He turns to me. 'He doesn't want you disappearing off again.'

Am I that obvious? 'Just give me a minute. I need to talk to Blake first,' I say.

Calum sneers as if there's no way that's happening.

'Yeah, just give us a minute,' says Blake.

Calum nods and starts retreating to the front of the restaurant. Good! As soon as he's out of sight, I'm going to jump on the moped. But to my horror, Jenks and Richie appear at the end of the road, gesturing for me to join them. Damn!

'Can you pick me up at eleven tonight?' I whisper. 'Everyone should be in bed by then.'

Blake stares at me in shock. 'You want *me* to sneak out?'

'Yeah,' I say, hurrying towards my stunt team.

Blake, please don't let me down.

CHAPTER
34

My alarm goes off and I jump out of bed, getting dressed as quickly as possible, when I realize there's movement and sound outside my door. Are people up? They should be asleep. I was going to creep through the house but it's got to be the window again.. Prising it open, I scramble through and land on my feet. I'm definitely getting better at this. I can't believe how light it is and then look up to see the full moon. That's great for my vision, but it also means other people can spot me. Keeping to the shadows of the walls, I creep around the house then dart to the perimeter hedge in the front garden, when I hear: 'Finn.'

You are kidding? Will this stop happening? Jerking around, I see Richie sitting on the doorstep, a bowl on his lap.

'Are you ill too?' he groans, before lowering his head and chundering.

I smell the vomit from over here. 'You're sick?' I say.

'We're all sick. It was the food at the Thai Orchid.'

I think of the Lingphi on the counter. Thank God I didn't eat anything. Clutching my stomach, I say, 'I was feeling ill too. I needed fresh air.'

'How did you get out?' Then he lowers his head and is sick again. 'Actually I don't care. Listen, you don't look that bad. Could you get me a drink of water?'

You want me to go back inside?

He looks up, green, clammy, and pitiful. 'Please, Finn.'

'I'm on it.'

I walk through the front door to find Jenks and Tom on the sofas, bowls beside them. Toilets are flushing from further inside.

'Is *everyone* ill?' I ask.

Jenks nods. 'What about you?'

'I'm not great, but I don't think I'm quite as bad as you lot. I'm getting Richie some water.'

I wait for him to ask me why I was outside, but he leans back and says, 'You're a saviour. Get me some too.'

Glimpsing my watch, I curse under my breath. What if Blake appears with Richie on the doorstep? I grab

Jenks and Tom drinks and hurry outside before Lucy and Calum can stop me too.

'Wouldn't you be better in bed?' I ask, handing Richie a glass.

'I think I might.' He takes a few gulps and staggers inside, the door swinging after him.

I look at my watch again. Blake is late—thank goodness. Then I curse again. What if he's not coming? What if he's decided— Then I hear the rumble of a moped and run down the path. Who cares if my stunt team notice I'm gone? Some things are more important.

'Sorry I'm late,' says Blake.

'I'm just glad you came,' I say, climbing onto the back of the moped.

Like most people in Thailand, neither of us bothers with helmets. I hold onto the back guard as Blake drives through the streets.

'Can't you go any faster?' I yell.

'I don't want to crash.'

Cos crashing is the worst thing that could happen right now!

'We need to swap,' I shout.

He speeds up a nanosecond and at last we get to the road of the sanctuary. I get him to pull over a little early so the engine doesn't wake up Charn Chi's parents and, more importantly, her sick grandmother. Then we run quietly over to the gate at the front of her house, not the one near the stables.

'We're going to have to go over the wall or the gate,' I whisper.

'I thought I was just giving you a lift.'

'But I'll need a lift home too.'

Blake scowls and then looks up to the top of the wall. 'I can't climb that high.'

I squeeze my jaw. He's got a point. We could be here all night waiting for him to scale it. 'All right, stay here.'

'On my own?'

'Do you have any other suggestions?'

'I go back to bed and you and Charn Chi deal with this.'

I throw him a look before scrambling over the gate. I drop onto the driveway on the other side and glance at the house. No lights are on, but I still bolt from tree to tree. I circle the house and realize I have no idea which room is Charn Chi's. I can't throw stones at her window; I'm going to have to go in.

Swooping onto the balcony, I stare through the window, then smile. There's no glass, just a hole in the wood. Poking my head inside, I scrabble with the curtains hoping to see a girl's bedroom, but I can't see a thing. *Aargh*. This could be anyone's room. I'm going to have to chance it. My aim is to dive into the room and roll quietly across the floor. My foot gets stuck in the curtain and I slam to the ground. I freeze.

Suddenly a shadow jumps out of bed. A knee is on my chest and a hand around my neck. I don't know who it is, but they're squeezing tight. My fist clenches and I'm about to punch, when a girl yelps, 'Finn, is that you?'

'Charn Chi,' I croak.

'What are you doing here?' she hisses.

'If you let go, I could tell you,'

'Oh, sorry.' Releasing me, she moves back silently.

I clear my throat as quietly as I can, rubbing my bruised neck, my eyes becoming accustomed to the darkness. 'That was some move.'

She shrugs. 'What are you doing in my room?' she demands.

'The Lingphi is still here.'

'What? Are you sure?'

'Well . . . he cut the brakes on my tuk-tuk during a stunt and I think he's given everyone food poisoning.'

'But that is impossible. He fulfilled my wish.'

'A lot of this seems impossible.'

She starts muttering in Thai and then stands up. 'Have you checked the offerings at the temple? Has he eaten them?'

'I didn't think to do that.'

'Come.' She pulls back the curtain and leaps outside, before grabbing the railing of the balcony and somersaulting to the ground.

'Have you ever thought about being a stunt woman?' I whisper.

She doesn't answer as she hurtles across the grass. I follow her and both of us stop beside the small yellow temple. The food has gone, only a few flies scavenging the remaining crumbs.

'Is this a trick? Did you eat it?' she asks, spinning around to look at me.

'Are you asking if I ate the maggot-infested fruit?'

Even in the moonlight I see her face drop and fill with fear. 'How do we get rid of him then?'

'I was hoping you could tell me.'

She crosses her arms and her words sound heavy. 'I am going to have to see Grandmother.'

'Isn't she sick?'

Charn Chi nods. 'And she is going to be very disappointed and angry, but we need help. She will have some idea.'

'She will?'

'I hope.'

Climbing back over the gate, I find Blake waiting for me.

'So? What's happening?' he asks.

'Charn Chi's talking to her grandmother.'

His face brightens. 'So we can go? It's their problem, right?'

'Blake, they might need our help. Charn Chi is meeting us back here. I told her you were with us too.'

Blake shudders and shakes his head. 'I should have just let you borrow my moped.'

Half an hour later he's still moaning and, I could kick myself. I should have just stolen it.

CHAPTER 35

'Finn,' whispers Charn Chi through the gate. 'Are you still there?'

Finally! 'What did your grandmother say?' I ask, leaning against the wood.

'She wants to see you and Blake.'

'Really?' Blake and I look at each other. 'Is she angry?'

'Not with you two.'

'You're going to have to open the gate then because Blake can't get over.'

'I thought he was an action hero.'

'That is why he has me,' I say, and Blake grimaces even more.

Two minutes later, Charn Chi returns with the keys

and opens the gates a fraction, making as little noise as possible. 'My parents are still sleeping,' she explains.

We hurry down the driveway and tiptoe up the external stairs. Kicking off our shoes, we follow Charn Chi into her house. As there are no curtains, the moonlight streams through the windows and illuminates the room. Almost everything is made out of wood—the walls, floor, and most of the furniture. Sculptures of mythical creatures and spiky potted plants decorate the sideboards, and an old woman sits in a chair, holding a handkerchief to her mouth. Blake clasps his hands together and bows his head and I copy him.

'Come,' she croaks, gesturing us closer. 'Which one of you is the seer?'

'I am,' I whisper.

It seems disrespectful to tower over her and so I kneel by her feet. Blake does the same.

She leans forward, searching my face. 'I have never heard of someone seeing a Lingphi when they have not summoned him. You must be an extraordinary boy.'

'I don't know about that.'

'I do.' She leans back. 'And now you must help my granddaughter. She has been very foolish.'

'She got the film location moved.'

'At what cost?'

I glance at Charn Chi. She's looking down, her fists clenched.

'Is there a way we can get rid of the Lingphi then?' I ask.

'There is. But it is dangerous.'

'Of course it is,' mutters Blake.

'When a Lingphi grows this strong, there is only one way to destroy it. You must'—her eyes bore into mine—'kill him.'

'Kill?' I yelp. Then clamp my hands to my mouth. I can't wake Charn Chi's parents.

'Once killed, the Lingphi will be reborn in hell and trapped . . . unless someone else reckless chooses to summon him.' She glares at Charn Chi who is thankfully not watching. 'I only know of one way to kill him. You must get the poison of the parrot flower inside of him.'

'He's got to eat it?'

She shakes her head. 'You must get it into his bloodstream. A poison arrow is the best way.'

'Wait! Did you say the parrot flower? Isn't that on Monkey Mountain?' Suddenly in my mind I'm back in the tuk-tuk with Richie. We're on our way to the vine stunt and he's pointing at a mountain, telling me how it's overrun with vicious monkeys.

Grandmother nods. 'I told you it would be dangerous.'

'Should we get some help?' says Blake. 'I could talk to my dad.'

'No,' she snaps, leaning forward again, but this time almost nose to nose with Blake. 'You must tell no one.

They cannot learn the secrets of the cave.' She starts to cough, her whole body shuddering.

Blake recoils, as I'm sure saliva lands on him. Glowering at Blake, Charn Chi speaks in Thai and strokes her grandmother's back. The woman stops coughing and looks at me.

'You must tell no one,' she repeats, and grasps my hand. Then she jerks back as if electrocuted, staring at me in wonder or horror. I can't work out which.

'What? What is it?' I say.

She grasps my hand again, clasping it in between both of her palms. 'I have never felt so much power running through someone before. Does the Lingphi keep coming back to you?'

'He seems to.'

'He senses your power. The Lingphi will see you as a danger and will stop at nothing to destroy you and all the people you love. Your family is not safe, including your brother.' She drops my hand and points at Blake.

'Oh, I'm not his brother. We just look alike,' says Blake.

Without thinking, I yelp, 'Blake's not safe? Which means Marcus isn't either. Or my mum.'

'None of you are safe. The Lingphi will travel this world hunting all of you down,' says her grandmother.

Blake grabs my arm. 'Why wouldn't I be safe? We're not brothers.'

Oh God!

'He's just my stunt double.' Blake's voice is mocking, incredulous. 'There's no way he can be my—'

We turn to look at each other at the same time. As soon as Blake sees my face, his eyes widen and his skin pales. I try to make my expression blank or disbelieving even—but I'm too late.

'No. NO! We can't be . . . can we?' He drops my arm, falling backwards onto his bum. 'Are we brothers?' he demands loudly.

Charn Chi slams her hand across Blake's mouth. 'Shh,' she hisses. 'My parents.'

He attempts to jerk out of the way, but Charn Chi keeps him in place.

Suddenly her grandmother tries to stand, holding onto the armrests for support. 'I should come with you to Monkey Mountain. I can help.'

'Grandmother, you cannot,' says Charn Chi.

I have to agree. She'd slow us down.

'You are children.'

'It's OK, we've got this,' I say, trying to sound more confident than I feel.

Charn Chi throws me a tight smile before returning her gaze to her grandmother. 'I caused this mess, I will sort it out, and I know exactly where the parrot flower is.' Then she looks at Blake. 'If I let you go, do you promise to keep quiet until we get out of the sanctuary?'

Blake nods, but his eyes are filled with confusion and, more worryingly, anger. He's going to speak—or more likely yell. I lift my hand ready to cup his mouth and silence him again, but when Charn Chi frees him, he says nothing.

Her grandmother falls back into the chair. 'Then I must thank you all and wish you good luck.'

We bow to her one more time before slipping out of the house.

At the bottom of the external stairs, Charn Chi says, 'I have got to get some things. I will meet you at the roadside.'

I don't take my eyes off Blake as we hurry through the gate.

As soon as we're on the other side, he turns to me and spits, 'Is it true? Are we brothers?'

'Yes,' I whisper.

'How?'

I hesitate. 'My mum and your dad.'

'Dad cheated on my mum?'

I nod.

'And you knew this and didn't tell me?' Blake clenches his fists.

I nod again, and step back, expecting him to punch me—I wouldn't blame him if he did. But he leans against the wall, his eyes growing wet. I feel tears well up in my eyes too, but we can't do this. Not now.

'Listen, Blake, I know this is huge for you to take in,' I say, scraping my hands through my hair. 'But I promise you—once the Lingphi is dealt with, I'll tell you everything I know. We'll sort it out. But right now I need you. The film needs you.' I take a deep breath. 'You're going to have to get over it.'

'Get over it?' he says through gritted teeth.

'Yeah. You've got about a minute.'

'A minute to get over the fact that—' His words drop away and he closes his eyes.

I watch his jaw clench, his pain obvious, and I wish I could do something about it. Then Charn Chi appears, wheeling her moped out of the grounds, two bulging carrier bags dangling from the handlebars.

'I got some bananas,' she says.

'That's what you've got, bananas? I thought you were going for a crossbow!' I sigh heavily, then turn to Blake. 'I'm so sorry, your minute's up.'

He wipes his eyes and nods.

CHAPTER
36

Blake lets me drive. In fact, I'm not sure he's even aware he's on a moped. He seems dazed—not that I blame him. *Please just keep holding on!* I know it's unfair of me expecting him to get over it so quickly, but we have no time. We have no choice. And we need him. Our plan is to get the flower and then work out how to shoot the Lingphi. We follow the road as it twists and turns through the rainforest, mountains sprawling either side, and soon we reach the base of Monkey Mountain. Charn Chi stops and I pull up beside her.

'Monkeys are day creatures so we have to hope they do not wake. But just in case—' She pulls the bags off the handlebars.

'So that's why you wanted bananas!' I say.

She grins. 'Nothing gets past you.'

'So . . . are we walking if we don't want to wake them up?'

'The parrot flower is right at the top and we would not get there by daylight if we walked. Plus this way we can make a quick escape if necessary.' She puts on some gloves. 'For the flower. Its toxins are deadly to humans too.'

This is getting better and better.

I glance back at Blake. 'Are you all right?'

He says nothing. I'm not sure he heard. 'I'll take that as a yes,' I say. 'Hold on tight.'

We climb the winding road, while looking out for monkeys. The mountain becomes steeper and the road narrower. Grass grows in the centre and soon we're on a track. Dodging holes and crumbling stone, I suddenly hear an animal screech. Looking left, my heart stops. It's like a scene from *Planet of the Apes* . . . except with monkeys. Lit up in the moonlight, hundreds of them dangle from trees, perch on rocks. They seem to have appeared out of nowhere.

Charn Chi must notice too because she speeds up. I twist the throttle and try to keep up, but with Blake weighing me down it's not easy. The monkeys swing from tree to tree and seem to be growing even larger in number, their shrieks filling the air. Then Charn Chi brakes and I come to a stop behind her. The monkeys freeze, no longer shrieking, their eyes glued on us. I hardly dare breathe. We're right at the top of the mountain and the air feels dangerous.

Charn Chi climbs carefully off her moped and the monkeys twitch but don't come any closer. She lifts the bags off her handlebars and tiptoes towards me.

'Once you take them out of the bag, whatever you do, do not keep hold of the bananas. You must throw them away from you as far as possible,' she whispers.

I nod. 'Did you get that Blake?'

'Yeah,' he says.

I look back at him and his eyes are no longer dazed, but terrified. Terrified I can handle. It means he's alert. I hand him the second bag.

'I am going for the flower,' says Charn Chi.

She takes a deep breath and steps off the pathway. It's as if she's declared war. Instantly the monkeys howl and swarm through the trees and off the rocks towards her.

'Here, monkeys,' I yell, grabbing a banana from the bag.

I wave it in the air. Their heads twist towards me and they hurtle in my direction. I lob the banana as far as I can and the monkeys leap on it, tearing at each other to get the fruit for themselves. I throw another and another. Blake does the same. Some monkeys leap closer, staring hungrily at the bag. One swings towards me, trying to grab it. I roar angrily and he jumps back for a second, then bares his teeth. He looks so much like the Lingphi, I just want to throw him the bag and get out of here. More monkeys circle us, getting braver, realizing where the bananas are coming from. We throw them further.

'Hurry, Charn Chi!' I yell. 'We don't have many left.'

'I have got it. I have got the flower,' she shouts, running towards us.

A monkey lands on her shoulder and she yanks it off, pushing it to the ground before leaping onto her moped. I chuck my last banana, rev the engine, and follow Charn Chi off the track as we U-turn. Then we both hit the path. Monkeys scamper after us and two leap onto my head, but somehow I keep hold of the handlebars.

'They're after the bananas,' screeches Blake.

'What bananas?'

'I have some left.'

'Then throw them!'

I want to kill him. I brake sharply. One monkey falls forward but the other clings to my hair. I feel like it's ripping chunks out of my scalp.

'Throw them,' I shout again.

'I have to get them out of the bag.'

I hear rustling and finally spot bananas flying through the air. The monkey jumps off me and others leap out of the trees fighting for the fruit. I twist the throttle, skid down the road, and at last we reach the bottom of the hill.

'What kept you?' says Charn Chi, her engine idle.

'Someone didn't get rid of their bananas,' I say through gritted teeth.

Blake looks livid. 'It's not as if you gave me a chance. You just started driving again and I had to hold on.'

OK . . . he has a point.

'You've got the flower?' I ask.

She holds open another plastic bag and, even though it's squished at the bottom, the petals still resemble a bird.

'It really looks like a parrot,' I say.

'What did you expect with a name like that?' she asks.

Suddenly I hear screeches and leaves rustling. 'Are they following us?'

Without waiting to see if they are, we race down the main road, passing mountain after mountain. At last we stop. The monkeys can't have followed us here. We've gone too far at too high a speed.

'So have either of you got any idea how you're actually going to do this?' says Blake, climbing off the moped. 'How you're going to shoot the Lingphi?'

Charn Chi bites her lip. 'We need a bow and arrow. I could try making them but it might take time, and I need bamboo, string, a pointy stone—'

'Or we could just borrow one from the prop department. Blake, does Marcus still have all the keys?' I ask.

He nods.

'Then we need to get the keys from your house and search the prop trailer.'

'And while you search it, I can mash up the petals, ready to coat the arrows.' Then Charn Chi's brow furrows.

'But . . . how are we going to find the Lingphi?'

I shake my head. 'We're not. He's going to find us.'

'What? How?' she says.

I lean forward on the moped, my arms folded over the handlebars. 'I was watching the monkeys, seeing how the bananas lured them away from you. And I thought: what could lure the Lingphi towards us? When does he appear the most?'

'When you are on an elephant?' says Charn Chi.

Blake's eyes widen. 'When you're doing a stunt.'

'Exactly. Pretty much every time I've done a stunt and put myself in danger, the Lingphi's turned up.' I push myself off the handlebars and sit up straight. 'We are going to create a stunt and do it in a place where Blake can get an easy shot of him.'

'Wait! Did you say me?' Blake jerks his head back.

'Do you honestly want me firing an arrow?' I say. 'Do you not remember how bad I was?'

'What about her?' says Blake, thumbing his hand at Charn Chi.

'I have never done it before,' she says.

Blake looks at her in surprise. 'But you knew how to make one.'

'I was guessing how to make one. They do not look that hard.'

I grab hold of Blake's arm. 'It has got to be you.'

'But I won't be able to see him,' he says, wrenching out of my grip.

'You will if I touch you, like after the tuk-tuk stunt.'

'Or I can touch you,' says Charn Chi. 'I told Grandmother how you saw the Lingphi when Finn touched you, and she said that happens sometimes. The sight can pass from the seer to a chosen one through touch.'

Blake shakes his head and steps backwards. 'I'm not a chosen one.'

'You're Blake Saunders, you're a sort of chosen one,' I say.

'You can't possibly want me to fire it,' he says, still shaking his head. 'You remember what my dad said—' his face twists '—our dad said. I'm not brave. I'm style over substance.'

I can't bring myself to call him 'Dad'. He hasn't earned that title. 'Marcus is wrong, Blake. You went to a tribe in Papua New Guinea. You helped capture and then release a Ropen.'

'Only because I had to.'

'You have to do this.'

'No, I don't. Dad's right. I'm no Rio. You are.'

'Then prove Marcus wrong.'

'After today, I'm not sure I even care enough about him to bother.'

'Then forget about him. Do this for you. Prove to yourself you can do it. You are not just style but substance too.'

Blake's eyes dart between the two of us. 'Say I agree, and I haven't yet, have you thought about the stunt?'

230

I feel the grin spread across my face. 'Now that I know Charn Chi can pass on the touch, I've got the perfect stunt and the perfect place. This is the plan . . .'

CHAPTER

37

We pull up on our mopeds beside the security gate; the bungalows and studios lie behind.

'I don't think security will care,' I say. 'They haven't asked me for ID yet.'

'We should go in together though, in case they stop me,' says Charn Chi.

We inch our mopeds towards the gate and I bow at the two men who climb to their feet. I wait for them to wave us through but one of them opens the door to the cabin.

'Can I see some ID please?' he says.

'Sorry?'

'ID please?'

'I forgot it. It's in my bungalow.'

The man looks at Blake behind me and at Charn Chi. 'Have the others got ID?'

My stomach squirms. 'They've forgotten theirs too.'

The man's eyebrows rise—*Yeah, I wouldn't believe me either*—when suddenly I feel Blake get off the moped.

'Do you know who I am?' he says with a slight edge to his voice.

The security guard tilts his head, then his eyes widen and his back straightens. 'Mr Saunders, I am so sorry. I did not recognize you for a moment. Please pardon my inexcusable behaviour.'

'It's fine,' says Blake, smiling and waving his hand casually. 'It's wonderful to see the security gate monitored so well. I shall let my father know.'

The security guard beams and ushers us through. Blake climbs behind me again and we drive straight to his house.

'Wow! Who knew?' I say, as we stop. 'Your obnoxious behaviour could actually be useful.'

'I'm here to help,' says Blake, grinning.

'Will there be any more security?' asks Charn Chi.

'I imagine there'll be guards wandering around the warehouses. We'll have to keep an eye out for them. Or Blake can do his: "Do you know who I am?"'

'Is he really that famous?' says Charn Chi, as we watch him disappear through his front door.

'Oh yeah.'

'And he is really your brother?'

Hearing someone else say it hits me like a wrecking ball . . . 'Yeah, he is.'

'But you are not famous?'

Does she want to kick me too? 'No, I'm not.'

She looks at me searchingly. 'Now I know, I can see that you are brothers. You are very similar.'

'In looks for this film. We're both Rio.'

'In personality too.'

Yeah, she might as well karate-kick me to hell. 'Don't you dare! We are nothing alike.'

She laughs, looking back at the front door. 'Do you live in a big house too?'

'Big enough.'

Come on, Blake, please come out. I don't think I can cope with any more of these questions. As if he heard me, the door opens and Blake hurries back up the path.

'My parents are awake,' he whispers, as soon as he reaches us.

'Now?' I look at my watch. It's 1.38 in the morning. 'Did they see you?'

'No. They were too busy throwing up.'

'Seriously? They have food poisoning too? Did your mum eat at the Thai Orchid?'

'She went there for dessert.'

I exhale deeply. 'The Lingphi was thorough, I'll give him that.' Then a horrid thought sneaks its way into my head. What if the Lingphi gave everyone lethal doses of food poisoning? What if they're—*No, I can't think like that!*

'You got the keys?' I ask, and Blake opens his hand revealing a labelled set.

He climbs behind me again and soon we're roaring along the road. We park our mopeds at the edge of the warehouses in the shadows of a building. Creeping on foot between the large storerooms, we head for the trailers.

'Do you know which one the props are in?' I whisper.

Blake nods. 'Dad took me there.' He stops behind a trailer, tapping the wall. 'It's this one.'

Charn Chi drops to her knees, opening her plastic bag and pulling out the flower. 'You two get the bow and arrows, while I turn this to pulp.'

'It seems a shame,' I say, looking at the beautiful parrot shape.

She glances up. 'Think of the Lingphi and all he's done.' And suddenly it doesn't seem that much of a shame.

Blake and I hurry around the front.

'You keep a lookout while I go inside,' he says.

'What? No! You should be lookout. This is my idea.'

'I've got the keys.' He dangles them in front of me. 'Stand over there and make sure no one comes.'

I look at him in shock. 'Who made you in charge?'

'I did. I am the older brother after all.'

'What?'

'I'm two months older than you,' he says, his lips twitching.

He turns around and fingers the keys, using the light on his mobile to find the appropriate label. Creeping over to where he suggested, I can't help but feel begrudging respect. Blake seems to be dealing with the news about his dad and me far better than I did.

I watch him slip through the door before I search for security or anyone else who happens to be about. The place seems empty. A few minutes later, Blake reappears and hurries over to me with a bow and quiver full of . . . two arrows?

'Is that it?' I whisper.

'That's all there was. They must have moved the rest elsewhere, probably to wardrobe.'

I groan loudly. 'We don't have time to look. We have to get this done before any film crew show up, and you know they like early starts.'

'Maybe we'll get lucky and they'll have food poisoning.'

'I'm not sure that counts as lucky.'

'Well . . . not for them.'

We run around the trailer to find Charn Chi scraping a stone against the petals or what used to be petals. Now they're a massive lump of poison.

'Have you got the arrows?' she asks.

'I could only get two,' says Blake, handing them over.

'Two are better than one.'

236

She rolls the steel points in the pulp, when I spot light flickering against a wall on a nearby building.

'A torch,' I yelp.

Charn Chi jumps to her feet, clasping the arrows, and we dart behind the trailer, flattening ourselves against the wall. I hear footsteps. Then a security guard walks past, about two metres away, his torchlight flying in all directions. He pauses close to us and lights a cigarette. *Seriously? Now?* He takes a few puffs and I can hardly breathe. Then thankfully he continues to another trailer. I let out a deep breath and hear the others do the same.

When his footsteps fade into the distance, I say, 'That was too close. We should get to the warehouse now.'

'They won't have dismantled it yet, will they?' says Blake suddenly.

'What?'

'They've begun taking down some of the sets as we're moving. They might have already—'

'Don't! Don't even say it.'

As if we could outrun their dismantling, we race to the warehouse. Blake fumbles with the keys, finally finding the right one. He opens the door and my heart soars. Yes!!! It's still there.

'I'll switch on the light once the door is shut,' I say.

'Will the light not show through the door?' asks Charn Chi. 'We do not want to alert security.'

Blake puts the keys back in his pocket. 'We should

be safe. When they soundproofed the warehouse, they made sure no light could get in, which means no light can get out.'

He closes the door and I flick the switch. We stare at the circular building in the centre of the room, with its external staircase leading to the viewing platform and the Wall of Death sign hanging off the front.

'So you two know what to do?' I ask.

Charn Chi nods. 'We are on the balcony. Blake is armed ready to shoot and I touch his shoulder. You ride the moped, and when the Lingphi appears and tries to sabotage the stunt, Blake shoots him.'

'Why does this seem like the most stupid of ideas?' says Blake.

'Because it is. But right now, I don't think we have a choice.'

'You know the Lingphi might not come.'

'He has to.'

'And I might miss.'

'You won't.'

I don't want to hear any more of Blake's doubts . . . because I have the same ones. We need to stay confident. 'Go upstairs,' I say.

While they climb the external steps, I find the door that leads to the bottom floor. I hurry inside and spot the bikes parked in the centre, keys in the ignitions. I grab the nearest and swing my leg over. Glancing up at the balcony, I see Blake holding the bow and arrow, Charn

Chi's hand on his shoulder. He looks like Rio in warrior mode as he scans the room.

'Finn does not have much space to drive,' says Charn Chi.

'He goes up the wall,' says Blake.

'He does what?'

'Well . . . he tries to go up the wall.'

'Thanks Blake! I can hear you.'

I know we're both thinking about my last attempt and suddenly I remember the shadow. It darted backwards like the Lingphi. Could the shadow have been the demon? If so, does the Lingphi ever come back to the same place twice? *Stop doubting yourself.* I have to be confident.

I turn on the engine and feel the bike's power.

CHAPTER 38

I kick the foot stand and twist the throttle. Circling the floor of the room, I keep glancing up at the viewing platform, looking out for the demon. Nothing. If the Lingphi's going to come, he's got to believe I could be in danger. I have to go higher. But what if I can't?

Trying not to think about my last attempt, I drive onto the ramp. I'm sure the Wall of Death is about confidence. Powering around the slope, there's still no Lingphi. Come on, just a bit higher. I put the wheel onto the vertical wall, and suddenly realize I'm driving horizontally. I'm doing it! I'm actually doing the Wall of Death. Why couldn't Marcus be here now? Why am I even thinking about him now?

I lift back my head to see Charn Chi and Blake waving their arms, cheering. At least I think they are. I can't hear them over the engine, over the wind. I raise my wheel a tiny bit more and I spiral up the wall. This is possibly one of the most daring stunts I've ever done. If the Lingphi's going to show, it will be to this one. Then my heart drops. What if he's decided he's not interested in stunts any more? What if he's only going to poison people from now on? My hands grow sweaty. Not the best idea on a bike. I try to take deep breaths, but the wind is roaring around me. Then something lands on my back. Claws reach over my shoulders. The Lingphi is here.

But his weight alters my balance and suddenly we're falling. I leap off the bike and somersault across the floor just as it crashes to the ground. At some point the demon must have jumped off my back because now it's charging towards me. I scoot backwards as Blake fires. The arrow races through the air . . .

The Lingphi twists and the steel point whizzes straight past him, clattering into the circular wall behind. Nooooo! Blake laces another arrow but the Lingphi turns his head. His eyes change from amber to gold and he scampers up the vertical wall as if he has sucker pads on his hands. He rips the arrow out of Blake's grasp and throws it like a dart, straight at me. I dive sideways and it hits the ground. My blood freezes. Blake's run out of arrows!

I watch in horror as the Lingphi whips around to face Blake again, his claws extending. The demon tears his hand across Blake's chest. Screaming in agony, Blake jumps back, jerking out of Charn Chi's touch.

'I can't see the Lingphi,' he shouts.

The demon swipes his chest again and blood splatters. I scramble to my feet, a roaring in my ears. *How dare he hurt my brother?* I make for the door—I have to get up there—when Charn Chi yells, 'Finn.'

I glance back round to see her snatch the bow from Blake's hands. She drops it over the edge and it slides down the wall. The Lingphi turns, his eyes following the bow. Charn Chi grabs the demon's arm, just before he can leap. He turns trying to bite her, scratch her. I race towards the weapon, swiping it into the air just as Charn Chi reaches over to touch Blake, making sure he can see.

'Help me,' she yelps.

Blake grasps the Lingphi's other arm. The demon wrenches his head left and right, snapping his teeth. Charn Chi and Blake throw him over the platform, while still holding on, so the creature dangles between them.

'Shoot him!' shouts Charn Chi.

My eyes dart about the room, landing on the arrows. I pick up the first, careful to avoid the poisonous end.

'Quick, we can't hold on much longer,' yells Blake.

The demon wriggles furiously, biting even more. My hands shake. This shouldn't be me. I'm an awful shot. And if I go wide, I could hit Blake or Charn Chi.

'Hurry,' yells Blake.

I lace the arrow and aim at the Lingphi, when suddenly his claws retract and his eyes grow big like some sort of Disney character or cuddly toy. He whimpers helplessly.

'Now,' shouts Charn Chi.

Remember he's a demon. Remember all the people he's hurt.

I pull back the string and release. The arrow whizzes through the air . . . straight for Blake. I swear loudly, but somehow Blake ducks, and the weapon flies over him, hitting the wall behind. I watch Blake reach behind, scrabble for the dart but it's out of his reach. And so I snatch the last arrow off the floor, my hands shaking even more.

'You can do this,' yells Blake.

But I almost killed you.

The Lingphi cackles and his face changes from innocent cuddly to the demon I recognize. His eyes glow amber then gold and he leers at me, knowing I'm rubbish. Twisting and turning his head, he snarls and bites, saliva dripping from his fangs.

I pull back the string. One shot. That's all I've got.

Sweat seeps into my eyes as I aim the point at the demon's chest. I take a deep breath and fire.

CHAPTER 39

The arrow soars through the room. The Lingphi squirms even more, snarling and screeching. The steel tip hits him in the stomach, piercing his fur and flesh. I stare in shock, not quite trusting that I did it. Then there's a desperate howl and blood oozes from the arrow. The Lingphi bursts into flames. Charn Chi and Blake shriek, releasing the fireball. I expect it to drop to the floor but the fire hovers in mid-air and seems to pulsate.

'We have to leave. NOW!' yells Charn Chi. 'Finn, get out!'

They disappear into the shadows seconds before the flames explode. I slam to the floor, my arms over my head. Peering up, I can't believe my eyes. A circle of fire spans the room, swirling and flickering a metre above me. The flames are brighter than I've ever seen. And they're getting closer, falling to the ground. Smoke billows and the stench of rotten eggs flies up my nose.

Remembering my training, I hold my breath and leopard crawl to the perimeter wall. I have no idea if I'm going in the right direction. I can't see through the smoke. The room's getting hotter and the flames are only centimetres above my head now. I reach the wall, but the fire's starting to scorch it. Where the hell is the door? Smoke burns my eyes and I need to breathe. I gasp for air and sulphuric smoke fills my lungs. I can't stop coughing when there's a rush of air.

'Finn, over here!' yells Charn Chi.

I turn to see her shadow standing in the doorway a little further down the circle. The flames begin to lick my back and I scream in pain. There's no point in crawling now. The fire's hit the floor. I scramble to my feet. Arms shielding my face, I follow her voice, stumbling through smoke and flames.

Blake pulls me out of the burning building. Charn Chi slams the door shut but I can see the fire spilling out of the roof now, the sign and external stairs in flames. I run for the door to the warehouse and whisk it open. Diving onto the grass outside, I roll over and over. Something's thrown over me and I feel hands pat my body.

'The fire's out,' says Blake breathlessly.

I lie still, hardly daring to move. My skin must have melted, my hair singed off. I should be in pain but the shock is taking over and I feel nothing.

'We should call the fire department,' I croak. 'We can't let that spread.'

'Actually Finn,' says Charn Chi, 'there is no need.'

'No need?' I sit up, and Blake's T-shirt falls in my lap. I turn to the open doorway and stare in astonishment. The flames have vanished. The roof, the walls and sign are all intact. The Wall of Death looks like it's never even seen a flicker of fire.

'What? How?'

'Look at yourself,' says Blake.

I peer down and in the moonlight, I see my clothes are dirty from the grass but they're not melted or burnt. There's not even smoke. Blake's T-shirt is on my lap. He must have taken it off to stop the flames. As I hand it back to him, I notice the holes and the blood.

'How's your chest?'

'I definitely have war wounds,' he says, his fingers tracing the scratches across his body. Thankfully they don't look as bad as I thought they would.

'Has the Lingphi gone back to hell then?' I say, turning to Charn Chi.

'I think so. I think they were the flames of hell swallowing it up.'

'I was in the flames of hell?' I fall backwards onto the grass. 'Did you know that would happen?'

She shakes her head. 'I had no idea. I do not think Grandmother did either or she would have warned us.'

'Someone's coming,' yelps Blake and suddenly I hear footsteps.

My stomach twists. The warehouse door is open and the light is on. Blake and Charn Chi must have the same thoughts, but their reactions are quicker than mine. As I stumble to my feet, they're switching off the light and closing the door as quietly as possible. We flatten ourselves against the wall. The security guard wanders past us, but doesn't aim his torch in our direction. I glance up at the sky. He's not going to need his torch much longer, which means the film crew could turn up at any moment.

'We have to go,' I say.

Keeping an eye out for security, we run past the warehouses until we reach our mopeds. But instead of climbing on them, we just stand there, looking at each other. Then Charn Chi laughs and clasps her hands to her mouth.

'We did it. We got rid of the Lingphi,' she says.

'We make one hell of a team,' says Blake.

'Can we not talk about hell just yet,' I say. 'That hell fire was just a little too close.'

We burst out laughing, the fear and tension melting away, when Charn Chi wraps her arms around me. I squeeze her back. For once, hugging a girl doesn't feel ridiculously awkward.

'Thank you for everything,' she whispers.

'You were amazing,' I say.

'I know,' says Blake, loudly. 'I was bloody marvellous.'

I step back, grinning. 'You were pretty good . . . although you did miss your shot and *I* hit the demon with the arrow.'

He rolls his eyes. 'That was beginner's luck.' Then before I can stop him, he climbs onto the front of the moped. 'Hey, little brother, I'll give you a lift home.'

I open my mouth to argue and then snap it shut. After all he's done for me, I reckon I can let him drive. Climbing onto the back, I turn to Charn Chi. 'You should let your grandmother know that we did it.'

She beams, her eyes sparkling. 'I cannot wait to see her face.'

We follow Charn Chi and I expect her to burn us off at the speed she drives, but to my surprise Blake keeps up with her. I think he might actually be turning into Rio. Halfway home, Charn Chi splits off, heading for the sanctuary, while Blake takes me back to the bungalow.

'Thanks for the lift,' I say, slipping off. 'In fact, like Charn Chi said, thanks for everything.'

'I think she was talking to you, Finn.'

'Well,' I shrug, 'I'm saying it to you.'

Blake smiles and then his face becomes serious. 'How long have you known?' he asks.

'Known what?'

He raises an eyebrow. 'How long have you know we're related?'

248

'We're doing this now?'

He folds his arms and I let out a long breath.

'I found out a few days ago. I heard your mum and dad talking.'

Blake leans over the handlebars. 'You know—this kind of makes sense. All those times he treated you like a son. Those times he cared more about you than me.'

'He never cared more about me, Blake. He felt guilty that I never had him around and that you had his time, his money . . . everything.' I hesitate. 'I know I have no right to ask you this, but is there any way you can not confront him just yet? I promised I wouldn't tell you, and he promised to get the film moved. He's stuck to his end of the bargain so I should at least look as though I stuck to mine.'

Blake turns away from me and stares into the distance. 'I'm not sure what I'd say to him anyway. But I am confronting him one day.'

'I know.' I let out another long breath. 'Blake, he does love you and he's very proud of you.'

'Oh, please, do not get all soppy on me.'

And I grin. Perhaps Charn Chi was right. Perhaps Blake and I are more alike than I thought and not just on the outside.

CHAPTER
40

I watch my brother disappear before heading to the bungalow. Jenks is going to kill me. Has there been a search party? I push open the door and instantly cover my mouth with my hands, the stench of sickness ripping through me. Jenks and Richie are lying on the sofas.

'I thought you were in your room,' says Jenks. Then he looks me up and down and his jaw drops. 'Where have you been? Is that blood?'

I glance down at my clothes. Oh no! They're muddy and covered in blood. Not my blood—it must be Blake's. I open my mouth, racking my brain for a reasonable explanation, when he shakes his head. 'Actually don't tell me. I don't want to know.'

I let out a deep sigh. 'Are you still feeling ill?'

'There should be a black cross on the door,' says Richie.

'Is everyone still ill?'

'Yep. But we've got to be better for the day after tomorrow,' says Jenks. 'We're moving location then.'

'So soon? I thought Strider wanted to film some more scenes here.'

'He's decided he can do them elsewhere. And I think everyone just wants to get out of here.'

*

'I still don't understand why the two of you didn't want to fly on a private jet,' says Richie. 'You could have at least let me take your place.'

'And me,' adds Lucy.

Blake and I are sitting amongst my stunt team at the back of a large coach filled with film crew. We've been on the coach for hours, travelling through Thailand to the second film location. I had no idea that the other underground cave Strider had in mind was at the opposite end of the country. Blake and I glance at each other. Neither of us is quite ready to face 'our dad' yet. Blake spent the day with me yesterday, keeping well clear of his house. Marcus and Natasha hardly noticed though, as they were still suffering. We visited Charn Chi and she was back to her sarcastic self—thank God.

'I wanted to see the countryside. If we'd travelled by plane, we would have missed it,' I say.

'I kind of wish you had taken the plane,' says Tom, looking at me. 'I'm not sure I want to be on this coach with you. I have never met such an unlucky person in my life. I think you really are cursed.'

'Hey, I'm the only one of the stunt team who didn't go down with food poisoning.' *And I'm not going to be unlucky any more!*

'Have you seen the footage of you in the tuk-tuk yet?' says Richie. 'Someone leaked it and it's gone viral.'

'Is Strider mad?'

'No. He's decided your near-deaths are fantastic publicity. This film is already making the headlines and it isn't even finished.'

'Attention-seeker,' mouths Calum.

I don't bother responding. Because as much as Calum annoys me, I know where he's coming from now. And I get it.

A phone pings and Blake pulls out his mobile. 'It's Dad,' he says, looking at me.' *Our* being the unspoken word. 'He's inviting you to come to a Thai boxing match with us. Do you want to come?'

Do I want to spend more time with Marcus?

I clench and unclench my jaw. 'Yeah, I would,' I say finally.

Blake smiles, messaging his dad—our dad—back. Then he turns to me and whispers, 'I'm trying to work out whether I should fire you as my stunt double.'

'What? Why? Cos now you think you can do your own stunts?'

'God no.' He pulls a face. 'And why would I want to? No—it's because whenever we film on location, you end up dragging me into a near-death experience.'

'You love it.'

'I really don't.'

'Yeah, you do.'

'No, I don't.'

Jenks hits the headrest in front of him. 'Oh my God, will you two shut up? You're like bickering brothers.'

Blake and I slam our mouths closed until I whisper, 'You love it, really.'

✳

At last we reach the hotel where we're staying and I stare in astonishment at the crowds lining the streets. Someone must have tipped off the public that the film crew are staying here.

'Blake, we're going to open the coach door,' shouts the AD from the front. 'Could you stand in the entrance and wave?'

'Sure,' says Blake, swaggering down the central aisle.

The door opens and he waves. Everyone starts screaming and chanting a name. All of a sudden my heart pounds. They're not shouting Blake. He turns to me just as amazed.

For the crowds are shouting, 'Finn, Finn, Finn!'

AN INTERVIEW WITH STUNT DOUBLE ANNABEL CANAVEN

1. HOW DID YOU BECOME A STUNTWOMAN?

I did performing arts at college, and went onto complete a dance degree at university. During this time, I got a summer job playing a squire at a castle. I watched the boys perform jousting and I thought 'I can do that'. So I started jousting in tournaments, playing Joan of Arc. Some of the jousters were also stuntmen and I thought—this is something I would love to do.

2. WHAT TRAINING DID YOU HAVE TO DO?

To be accepted onto the JISC joint industry stunt committee you have to take tests in the listed disciplines. Mine are Taikwando (I'm a black belt), horse riding, trampolining, climbing, swimming, and high diving.

3. HOW LONG DID IT TAKE TO TRAIN?

It took me about two years but I could already horse ride and trampoline to a high level and these were two of my tests.

4. WHAT CHARACTERISTICS DO YOU NEED TO BE A STUNT PERFORMER?

Be an all-rounder. Be enthusiastic, fit, flexible. Brave but not stupid. You really have to look after yourself, physically and mentally. Your body is your tool and you have to keep in good shape.

5. ARE YOU SCARED BEFORE THE STUNTS?

Adrenalin always runs through me. Sometimes I'm scared to do the stunt, but it's not fear of the action scene. It's the fear that I could mess up. I don't want to ruin the shot.

6. WHAT FILMS AND TV SHOWS HAVE YOU BEEN IN?

I have been in so many film and TV programmes; these are a few of my favourites—*Harry Potter and the Deathly Hallows Part 2, Skyfall, Suffragettes, Everest, Doctor Who, Maleficent, Thor: The Dark World, Great Expectations, Cockneys Vs Zombies, Call the Midwife, Wolfblood, Jonny English Reborn, Nanny McPhee Returns, The Woman in Black 2,* and *Kingsman: the Secret Service.*

7. WHAT IS YOUR FAVOURITE STUNT?

I love working with horses. It's great to gallop on beautiful well-trained stunt horses who are trained to rear and lie down as well as many other tricks. Plus I really like fire or being underwater. It's almost meditative for those few seconds the fire is building around you—you can hear the flames and feel the warmth. And underwater, you are in the zone.

8. WHAT WAS YOUR SCARIEST STUNT?

Being jerked out of the back of a moving van. There was no warning. One second I'm standing in the back, waiting. The next I'm being dragged behind the van.

9. DOES IT HURT?

Yes!!!! But it depends on the stunt and if you get to wear pads or not, and how many times you have to do the same stunt. The adrenalin keeps you going during the filming, but the next day you can be sore all over.

10. WHERE HAVE YOU BEEN ON LOCATION?

Belfast, Iceland, Scotland, Wales, England and Greece

11. HAVE YOU EVER WORKED WITH ANYONE WHO WANTS TO DO THEIR OWN STUNTS?

It depends on what the stunt is! But yes, actors can do their own action scenes. The set-up of the stunts and rehearsals are always with the stunt performer. Then at the last minute for the actual shot—the actor is used.

12. WHAT IS THE BEST THING ABOUT BEING A STUNTWOMAN?

Not only do you get to play lots of different characters—you can be anyone—you're also in some of the most exciting parts in films and TV. People from other film departments come out to watch your scenes as they are exhilarating and dangerous.

13. WHAT IS THE WORST THING ABOUT BEING A STUNTWOMAN?

The wigs!!! They're tied to your hair with hundreds and hundreds of pins. Plus the costumes can sometimes be tight and uncomfortable, especially if you have to squeeze padding or jerk vests underneath them too. Often the actors are very slight and I am more muscly. I have ripped many, many costumes on set before. Also there is a lot of hanging about for when they want you to do your scene.

14. WHAT DO YOU DO TO KEEP FIT?

I do a lot of cardio such as swimming and running. I also have to keep my skills up in gymnastics, trampolining and weapon training.

15. WHAT IS YOUR DREAM FOR THE FUTURE?

To work in New Zealand; it's such a beautiful country, and my niece and nephew live there! As well as doubling Ariel if they ever make a live action of *The Little Mermaid*.

16. WHAT ADVICE WOULD YOU GIVE SOMEONE WHO WANTS TO BE A STUNT PERFORMER?

To train hard and learn to act. Performing is huge part of the job. Plus, be versatile. A stunt performer is a job for an all-rounder as you need to have so many skills.

ABOUT THE AUTHOR

Tamsin loves to travel, have adventures and see wild animals. She lives in Somerset with her adrenalin-junkie family and soppy dog. She likes the idea of being a stunt double, but isn't that brave . . . so writes about them instead!

THE STUNT DOUBLE
BOOK LAUNCH
2017

THE SCARLET FILES SERIES

STUNT DOUBLE SERIES

ACKNOWLEDGEMENTS

One person may write a story but it takes a whole team to create a book, and so I would like to thank all those amazing people who have helped me.

This book wouldn't be here—no scratch that—I wouldn't be here if it wasn't for my wonderful agent Anne Clark. She is always there for me, offering support, encouragement and guidance.

The whole team at OUP have been fantastic. My editors, Clare Whitson and Gill Sore, have pushed my writing, brainstormed wonderful ideas and helped me make Jungle Curse the best it can be. And once again, Lizzie Smart has created a wonderful cover. I love how Finn swings from the vines, and the jungle scene really draws you in.

Not only am I lucky enough to have a team of publishers supporting me, I have a fabulous family around me too. Graham, my husband, has read countless versions of my stories, offering great insight. I'm not sure that was in our wedding vows but he has always stepped up to the plate. And my children Toby and Daisy have endured endless questions around the dinner table, such as: 'So . . . if you were riding a stampeding elephant—what would you do?' They are definitely the inspiration behind the teenage characters.

I'd like to thank my dad for being my greatest cheerleader. Most importantly, he read stories to me when I was little, instilling the love of books that I have today. My sister Pia, and I used to tell each other stories as well, pretending to be in *Jackanory*. Now we are both writers, and together we can share the joys and pains of writing! Mum, you might not be here, but you always believed in me.

So a huge thank you to all my family.

There are also some friends who deserve a special mention. Helen Jones for coming over at short notice to help with plot holes and Anne Inge for making me Jerk vests. Ruth Wallbank, Floss Clarke, Eileen Flude, Charlotte Loxston, Nic Hill and Sophie Holm for their never-ending support and love.

I'd like to thank Booklover Jo for supporting my books. She's also invited me to her school, where I've met fabulous children. Definitely a few Finns in there! Also I am so grateful to Kate Poels and Miss Cleveland for being such great champions of Stunt Double.

I'd also like to thank Marcus Bishop and his team at Waterstones in Yeovil, who have really helped promote my books and put on fantastic launches.

I'm incredibly grateful to Annabel Caraven. She is such a cool stuntwoman, who has told me so much about stunts and who I now consider a lovely 'mad' friend. Plus Andreas Petrides who runs the British Action Academy. Thank you so much for letting me spend the day with you and your students. You're all much braver than me! And I'd like to thank Mike James for teaching me all about motorbikes. Like I said in Book One, if there is anything incorrect in this book, please don't blame anyone mentioned here. I am an 'arteest' and may have taken some dramatic license.

I'd also like to thank the Hutsadin Elephant Sanctuary in Hua Hin, Thailand, where I met amazing volunteers and fabulous elephants, including one who loved to have her tongue stroked.

And finally to my readers. I really hope you enjoyed this next instalment of Finn's adventures.

TURN THE PAGE TO READ THE FIRST CHAPTER FROM
SCARLET FILES: CAT BURGLAR

CHAPTER ONE

I lie flat against the edge of the roof, my senses on high alert. Come on, Dad, where are you? Surely it shouldn't take this long to see if a room is clear. Then a hand clutches my shoulder and my body jumps. Somehow I manage not to fall off the three-storey house. I stare at Dad in amazement. How can he be so quiet? I haven't heard a footstep or even a scuffle on the tiles.

Dad swoops over the lip of the roof, dropping to the second-floor balcony below. This is it—the moment I've been waiting for. I take a deep breath and scramble over the guttering. With fingers clinging to the roof, I dangle nine and a half metres above the ground. Adrenalin surging, I swing my legs and hurtle through the air before landing, knees bent, beside him. I rub my arms and stretch out my fingers.

1

Dad and I are dressed the same—black overalls, balaclavas, thin leather gloves, and rucksacks. Our night-vision goggles make the world green. Together we stare through the glass double doors. The room in front of us is empty, but the owners are sleeping in the next bedroom. Have we woken them? I hate to admit it, but my landing was much louder than Dad's.

Thankfully no lights appear, and Dad picks the lock in the door. Reaching into my back pocket, I pull out a sliver of foil. I hand it to Dad and watch him use it to block the sensor. He slides the door open a fraction, and when the alarm doesn't go off, he yanks it further on its rails.

Dad creeps into the house first and I follow closely behind. He shuts the balcony door, while I take stock of the room. Everything is exactly where I expect it to be—the double bed, the rug, the chest of drawers, the mask, and the jewellery box. Dad's plans were perfect.

I step forward when Dad grabs hold of my arm and jabs his index finger at the large oval rug. My mouth dries. I can't believe I forgot. I give him a quick thumbs-up.

We grab the edge of the rug and carefully roll it back, to reveal small pressure pads dotted about on the carpet. If I'd stepped on one of those, an alarm would have exploded somewhere. Most of the pads are clustered below the spot where the Aztec mask is hanging. Even through my night-vision goggles, the mask looks horrible, frightening. I'm not sure how anyone could sleep with that thing staring down at them.

I watch Dad navigate the room. He pulls some tweezers out of his bag and starts fiddling with various wires. While he deactivates an alarm attached to the mask, I tiptoe across the carpet, avoiding the few pressure pads in my path. My target, the jewellery box, is on top of the chest of drawers. According to Dad's plans, the box is free from alarms, but I finger the area just in case. Good—there are no wires or signs of extra security.

Tilting the wooden lid, I find the box stuffed with brooches, bracelets, and necklaces. I ease some of it to one side when I hear a noise. I freeze. There's another noise—a creak. Someone, somewhere in the house, is moving. I hardly dare breathe. My eyes dart between the door to the landing and Dad, who stands motionless with the Aztec mask in one hand. Dad lifts his free hand, holding it out in front of him. I know what he's telling me: Don't panic. Don't move.

I stay still. Feet scuff the carpet on the landing. Now should we bolt? Again I glance at Dad, but his hand remains in the air. The footsteps pass our door, but that doesn't mean we're safe. What if it's someone collecting a cricket bat to bash us over the heads with? Or phoning the police? I hear a click, and a soft glow of light appears from under the door to the landing. Then I catch the sound of tinkling. I let out a quiet sigh. It's just someone going to the toilet.

Still I don't move and neither does Dad. The tinkling seems to be endless. Finally, I hear a chain flush and a click, and the glow disappears. The footsteps begin again, passing our room, and a bed creaks as someone climbs into it. Dad's hand is still flat against the air. My muscles ache from being so tense. I know he's waiting for the person to fall back to sleep. But really? Do we have to wait this long? At last Dad changes his flat hand into a thumbs-up and twists back around.

As quietly as I can, I dive back into the jewellery box, this time rummaging with more speed. Soon my eyes fall upon a thick bracelet covered in precious stones and I can't contain my grin. I've found it! Fingers shaking, I lift the bracelet, wrap it up in a square of black velvet, and slip it into the front pocket of my rucksack. I pull out an exact replica and stuff it in the bottom of the box. Then I carefully pile on the rest of the jewellery, trying to remember the order in which I took it out. A beaded necklace and dragonfly brooch were definitely on the top. I close the lid, and wipe down every surface I touched. Stepping back, I examine my work. No one will notice . . . hopefully.

I turn around to see Dad reactivating the alarm, now attached to a fake mask hanging on the wall. He wipes down the whole area before hopping over the pressure pads. I meet him by the double bed and together we unroll the rug. Dad studies the room and nods. He uses the foil to stop the sensor, and signals for me to open the door. Slipping outside, I wait for him to join me out on the balcony.

I feel lightheaded. The tension drains away. I can't believe I stole the bracelet . . . all on my own!

4

Dad relocks the glass doors, as I hoist the rucksack onto my shoulders. Together, under the moonlit sky, we climb over the railings and swing onto the first-floor balcony. Without pausing, we leap over another set of railings and drop to the ground. No streetlights—we run to our black car and jump inside.

Dad drives two streets away, before saying, 'NVGs.'

I tear off my night-vision goggles and Dad does the same. He puts on the headlights.

'So what do you think? How did I do?' I burst.

'You were great,' says Dad.

I clasp my gloved hands together. 'When can I do it again?'

'Soon,' says Dad. 'But right now, I think you should try to get some sleep. After all, you do have school tomorrow.'

CHAPTER TWO

Next morning, the lessons drag and I'm finding it hard to keep my eyes open. At last the bell rings for lunch. I grab my sandwiches, head to the canteen and sit at the far end of a table. As usual empty chairs surround me.

A group of girls fall into the seats at the table behind, laughing and chatting. My heart reels. That would have been me a year ago. I'd have been sitting with Jules and Charlie at my old school, laughing about something stupid. But I haven't seen them for ages. When Dad and I moved, I had to say goodbye . . . and I gave them a fake address. They think I'm living in South Africa. Tears start to prick the corner of my eyes.

Then I give myself a shake. It was my decision to join Dad on his mission. I knew what I was getting into—that I'd have to be cut off from my old life. I push my old friends to the back of my mind, and take another bite of sandwich, when I hear a voice from the table behind.

'You won't believe what I did last night!'

I glance over my shoulder to see a girl grinning madly. I turn back around but her voice drifts over loud and clear.

'Honestly, I had the most amazing night,' she says. 'Andy came over. And we stayed up till like three in the morning and watched two horror films.'

'You didn't?' squeals one of her friends.

'Yeah. Mum and Dad had gone out so . . .'

My lips can't help twitching. Seriously? Watching two horror films with a boy is *amazing*? Thinking about my night, my lips twitch even more. It was the first time Dad allowed me to take an item. Of course I've been on jobs before but I've always been his assistant—holding tools, being lookout, climbing through air vents. But last night he let me locate the bracelet, search for alarms . . .

I fiddle with my hair, reliving every last detail, when all at once I freeze. Something's wrong. The canteen's quiet. I look up and to my horror see that the room is empty. How long have I been here?

The bell rings and I jump to my feet. I can't be late for a lesson. The teachers will notice me. Running down the long hallway I arrive outside my classroom. Thank God I'm not the last one. Joining the stragglers, I drop quietly into my seat in the middle of the room.

Our geography teacher, Mr Anchor, starts droning on about rocks and I try to listen. Leaning on my elbow, I watch him write some geological words on the electronic whiteboard. My eyelids grow heavy, my body warms, my head lowers and before I know it, I'm in the world of dreams.

'Boring you, am I?'

My head jerks up. Mr Anchor is standing directly in front of me, his arms folded. My stomach hits the floor.

'I'm sorry,' I croak. I clear my dry throat. 'I'm sorry,' I say again, sharper this time.

'You've been drooling,' he snaps.

The class bursts out laughing and they strain to look at me. I drop my head and my hair falls over my face. I can't believe this is happening. After a year of making sure I blend into the background, I'm becoming the centre of attention.

'We're reading pages ninety-two to ninety-eight. Do you think you can do that? Or are you likely to fall asleep again?' asks Mr Anchor.

'I can do that,' I mutter, opening my book and flicking through the pages.

'Good!' he says, before returning to the whiteboard.

I avoid looking at anyone; afraid I might catch their eye. I could kick myself . . . or Mr Anchor!

Normally my classmates and teachers don't bother with me. I've made sure that I'm average in lessons, not in the top set or bottom. Even though I've missed a few days staying in safe houses, I've never skipped too much school to be noticeable. I have mousy hair, never wear make-up, and when I'm not in uniform, I dress in plain regular clothes. I haven't made any *real* friends here because I can't let anyone get too close. And to be honest, I find other thirteen-year-old girls pretty boring these days. All they seem to be interested in is music, clothes, make-up, and boys. I like hotwiring cars, defusing alarms, and cracking safes.

For the rest of geography I make sure I pay attention, but I keep an eye on the clock. Come on, 3.15! Eventually the lesson finishes and I grab my bag. Thank God it's the weekend. And after that, I only have two more days of school until it's the summer holidays.

I hurry home to find Dad in the kitchen, with a telephone glued to his ear.

'Sorry,' he mouths, his eyes darting skyward.

By Dad's scowl I know he's talking to his boss, Mr Higgs. Dad works for the magazine *Safe as Houses*. He researches all the latest anti-intruder technology and writes reviews on them. It's his perfect day job.

Leaving Dad to it, I climb the stairs to my room. As ever, it's perfectly tidy; my books stacked in height order; my desk clear of everything apart from the homework I didn't do yesterday; my bench-press loaded with the correct number of weights. Then I notice the corner of a blue scrapbook, peeping out from under my bed. Didn't I put it away properly? If Dad's seen it, he'll kill me. But as I drop to my knees, I relax. Dad never comes into this room.

I'm about to push the scrapbook further under the bed, when my hand hovers. Surely I can take another look. Just one.

Opening the book at the first page, I read the headline: *'Police baffled as Invisible Burglars strike again.'* The newspaper clipping is dated six years ago, when I first found out what Mum and Dad did. Since then I've kept all articles about them . . . and now about Dad and me.

The familiar pang in my chest returns as I think of Mum. She'd brush my hair, and tell me about their heists; how she used glasscutters, how she picked locks. I bite my lip. I reckon I could do some of those things now . . .

Flicking through the pages, I search for the clipping of her last heist, when there's a knock at the door.

My hand freezes.

'Scar, can I come in?' calls Dad.

You're kidding! Dad wants to come into my room? *Now?* I shove the scrapbook under my bed and grab my English homework before leaping onto the top of the duvet, as if I was sitting here all along.

'Scar, can I come in?' he calls again, louder this time.

'Sure.'

Dad walks in with a large bag dangling from one hand and a medicine box full of insulin for his diabetes in the other. He must have just injected. I glance up at his face. He looks serious. Oh no! He's seen the scrapbook!

'Is everything OK?' I ask, waiting for the explosion.

He rubs his forehead, then says, 'How was school?'

Of all the things I expected him to say, this was the last. We don't tend to talk about anything other than, well . . . cat burglary. 'I fell asleep in Geography,' I say, with a shrug.

'Oh?' says Dad, dropping into the chair at my desk. 'I guess that's my fault. Another late night.'

'I don't mind.'

'I know *you* don't. But your mother would.'

I glance at the only photograph in my room on top of my bedside table: the one of Mum with her arms around me. We're wearing matching T-shirts and caps with the logo for Born Wild on them. She used to work for the animal charity and I helped her whenever I could.

'She would have been proud of you,' says Dad. 'You did well last night.'

'I did?'

'You know you did!'

My face splits into a grin.

'You were a real professional,' he continues. 'You didn't panic when that person got up, you waited, and you—'

'Actually Dad, I've been thinking. I was wondering if I could start doing a bit more.'

His eyebrows rise.

'I could do a job on my own, just a little one. You could stay in the car. I'd pick the locks, get the items, and—'

'Scar, it's one thing to collect an item on your own. It's a whole different dimension, breaking into a house on your own.'

'But—'

'We've been through this before. You're too young, you're not ready and you've got much more to learn.'

I open my mouth to speak but Dad lifts his hand to silence me. 'Anyway, I need a favour. That was Higgs on the phone and he's on his way here with some burglar alarm for me to look at. I need you to put these things into the safe.'

He opens his bag, and pulls out the mask and bracelet from last night. I want to argue with him. I want to let him know that I'm more than ready to do a job on my own, but I can see from his expression it would be pointless.

'Fine,' I say with a sigh, taking the bracelet and mask from him. I'm surprised how heavy they are. I hadn't noticed yesterday. 'Are these really Aztec artefacts?'

Dad nods. 'From the 1500s.'

'Wow!'

'Wow indeed! They were stolen from a Mexican temple a few years ago. It's time they went back.'

I stand up, ready to move into the lounge, when Dad's watch beeps and a red light flashes on and off. The outside sensors have been activated. Someone is on our driveway.

'I don't believe it. That must be Higgs. He must have been on his mobile in the car,' says Dad, pressing a button on his watch, stopping the alarm. He grimaces at the mask and bracelet. 'You don't have time to get these into the safe. You're going to have to look after them here in your bedroom.'

'Will that be all right? I mean . . . will this be secure enough?'

Dad glances around. 'You know what? This room is probably the best place in the house. Higgs won't come in here.'

The doorbell rings and he throws me a thin smile before leaving the room. I hear him open the front door and start speaking. His words are muffled. I don't bother straining to hear what is being said. Instead, I wander in front of the floor-length mirror and hold the Aztec mask to my face. Why would anyone want this? It's horrible!

The mask is made out of wood, shaped like an over-sized human skull. The eyes are big black circles, surrounded with white shell. Holes have been cut out of the middle of each of them, and with my eyes peeking through the whole thing looks sinister.

The rest of the mask is covered in a mosaic of turquoise stones. Some are missing. Most are cracked. In the centre of the forehead is a deep hole where a larger stone must have once lived. A jewel perhaps? There's a leering mouth with . . .

My heart jumps. Are those *real* teeth? Was this mask made from *real* animal teeth?

I quickly put the mask on my desk and look at the bracelet instead. It's far more beautiful, but then, that isn't hard! It's a bangle, an inch thick and slightly mis-shapen, as if someone has tried to crush it in their fist. It's made out of finely woven gold, like spun silk, and has five bright turquoise stones running around the out-side. Each stone, the size of a twenty-pence piece, has been shaped into a creature. One resembles a bird with large wings, but I can't make out the others. They're too abstract, with bumps that could be legs or tails. It's weird that this bracelet is five hundred years old. The turquoise and gold look far too shiny and new, especially compared to the stones on the mask.

Without thinking, I slip my hand through it. I lift my arm into the air and the gold and turquoise seem to shine even brighter. I can't believe I found this in a box full of ordinary jewellery. It's too precious and valuable. In fact, it's so precious and valuable I should take it off.

I grab hold of the bracelet and pull, expecting it to slip off as easily as it slipped on. Yet the bracelet doesn't move. I yank again, harder this time but still it refuses to budge. Each time I pull, my skin is dragged with it. I stare closely at the bracelet. The gold is now flush against my skin. How is that possible? It was bigger than my hand seconds ago.

Then all of a sudden, I feel pain, as if sea urchin spines are stabbing my skin. I want to scream, but I can't. Dad's boss is in the lounge. I clamp my lips shut and try to pry my fingers under the gold. I want to pull the bracelet away, but my nails can't get an edge . . . there is no edge. The gold is sinking into my skin. The throbbing intensifies and I scratch frantically at my wrist. The gold is getting paler, the turquoise more translucent.

Then my stomach crumbles. For the bracelet vanishes completely. The pain stops, but I feel dizzy, weak. I fall backwards onto the bed, my body growing clammy. I lie there motionless. How long I lie, I'm not sure. At some point I hear a knock on the door but I can't even open my mouth to speak.

'Thank goodness Higgs has left,' says Dad stepping into the room. Instantly he's beside my bed. 'Scar, what is it? Are you ill?'

I feel the back of his hand against my head, but my eyes refuse to focus.

'Scar, what's wrong?' he demands.

At last I manage to open my mouth. In a small croaky voice, I say, 'The bracelet. It's gone.'

Ready for more great stories?

Try one of these...